## *Tell Her You Love Her*

Bridget O'Connor was born in London. She won the *Time Out* London Writing Competition in 1990 and her work has appeared in numerous magazines and anthologies, including *The Picador Book of Contemporary Irish Fiction*. Her previous short-story collection *Here Comes John* is also available in Picador.

*Also by Bridget O'Connor in Picador*

# *Here Comes John*

# *Tell Her You Love Her*

## Bridget O'Connor

**PICADOR**

*A Picador Paperback Original*

First published 1997 by Picador

an imprint of Macmillan Publishers Ltd
25 Eccleston Place, London SW1W 9NF
and Basingstoke

Associated companies throughout the world

ISBN 0 330 34290 8

The following stories have previously been published:
'Enquiries (General) in *The Printer's Devil*;
'Hearts' in the *Irish Post*;
'Heavy Petting' in *Psychoactive Synch*, Serpent's Tail.

1 3 5 7 9 8 6 4 2

A CIP catalogue record for this book is available from
the British Library

Typeset by CentraCet, Cambridge
Printed and bound in Great Britain by
Mackays of Chatham plc, Chatham, Kent

*For Feli,*

*Rosanna and Amaia Portelli,*

*with love*

## Acknowledgements

I'd like to thank the K. Blundell Trust, the London Arts Board, the Tyrone Guthrie Centre and Linda Adams of the Muswell Hill Bookshop.

I'd also like to thank my agent, Derek Johns, for his support.

Also my brother James for his sarcastic deconstructions, my sister Peggy for the cash injection, Jake for the medical advice and my chauffeur Margaret Quigley for all the drinking and driving.

# Contents

# *Lenka's Wardrobe*

What you'd probably like to hear is I get some kind of come-uppance. The baddy slips out from the shadows. I'm looking up the hole-nostrils of his gun. *Ba-bang!* I turn into Lenka. I'm haunted. The teddy bear runs off with the Barbie doll. Sinead comes back and beats me up. This ain't a laminated story with an ending like that. (Though, if you're interested, say, in making a film, like bio of my life . . .?) I get away with it. I stay pretty, rich.

And each morning off I belt to work.

*

'Eve, you're looking . . . really *different* lately.'

'Eve, have you had some kind of *make-over*?'

'Miss Carson, may I say you're looking particularly pretty this morning?'

You may.

I sashay to my desk and sit down. Grin.

*

Where I work, and this is like being *polite* about it, it's a Publishing House, call it a bungalow, on the Holloway Road (call it holding the phones). Call it biding my time. In the bungalow there's a stagnant pond full of dying fish going round and round: BIG gloopy red lips; knackered glam. I'm a PR girl. I sit in the pool with the other dying knackered girls. I keep my earrings in a glitzy pyramid next to my fags; my boy-traps (stack of cream cakes, gold pound coins), on full bait, for the roadrunners, the pizza-delivery kids. I seat myself at enticing angles, chat. As I have my mum's natural gifts, I see our dark-red iceberg auras bash about in the computer flash air. I *look after* (my italics) two prolific (no-life), BIG-WRITING, highly laminated crime writers, Carla and Jack. I send C&J – and their many aliases, and their many alter egos – yip-yapping off to Hemel Hempstead, Arlington, Lancaster and Morecambe. Bromley-by-Bow. I put them up in B. & B.s and plot their train routes for maximum grief. For a laugh, snorting half a line, hacking over my shoulder, Look, girls, ha ha! I punch glossy schedules out on the AppleMac. I stipulate my clients must receive a full macrobiotic diet. Listen, hag in Hove, *I'm stipulating*. Yeah, it's a scream.

Well, that's the kind of PR Princess I am. *Was*. Till Lenka moved in.

And each evening off I belt down the Holloway Road, through the Hackney Marsh, to my Leyton Palace home.

*

Leyton. A sandblasted land. Where else? It gets good evening sun. A great sprawl of burnt bathing-beauty sky. It goes pink and gold plated. Navy blue. Where else would a girl want to live? The stars come out like silver blinking crosses. Pubs dot it. Cars clog it. In winter, black limbless trunks wrist up it. In summer, leafy branches splash right across it. Lorries thunder through it at all hours, like trains. Helicopters (even) police above it. It's a sandblasted Palace on Palace Row, near the ice rink, down the canal. I inherited it from my ex. I really, I can tell you, *earned* it. After work, after a day grinning, bleeding *Personally Relating*, me and Sinead'd sit out here, knackered, on the front steps, chilling out in our leafy sarongs and bikinis, getting grit in our pina coladas, till the sky went gold plated, rose tinted, chalky blue ... The street lamps and the stars flicked on. We'd have a laugh, get wrecked, pose for the helicopter boys, blow (friendly) abuse out at the boy gangs and girl gangs (not so much cruising as clumping); at the little smoky Asian kids gliding by like trick or treat ghosts; at DIY Derek next door, flipping head over heels up ladders, like one of them wind-blown toys, spraying down sparks. 'What the *hell*,' we'd yell, 'what the bleeding hell you *doing*, Del?' Sinead does this wicked imitation: 'Just a spot of late night welding, girls.'

In winter, when it snows, this street looks real beautiful for about one hour. Whitely blue like Christmas-card glitter. You can hear Bing Crosby hum. You can see ice flowers crack the bay windows ... Sinead used to wander out happy-drunk in her cloak, our tennis rackets tied to her shoes, snorting hiccuppy laughs. A fat ginger-headed crow. Me and Sinead: ex-Princess-in-Chief, ex-Ginger-co-star. Near perfect harmony. Like seven years. Like, bleeding, really, Shangri-La nirvana. Till Lenka moved in.

Work. Clubbing. Clubbing. Work. We only advertised when we had nothing left to wear.

WANTED: THIRD PRINCESS FOR LEYTON PALACE.
MUST BE SOLVENT, FAT AND FIT.

(Must have a line in twinsets, lingerie, shoes or fifties suits. Must buy new clothes *all the time* . . .) Must be a bit, really, bleeding thick. Life was a constant costume change. Me and Sinead had a vacancy. OK, we nearly always did.

* * *

We'd been interviewing all day.

Enter Lenka.

'What an *extraordinary* colour,' Sinead said, our signal for, O my Jesus, *yuck*!

Sinead shot in first through the living-room door bulging her cheeks at me like they were filling with sick. I saw something in the hall, in a . . . *bolt* of poison-green. Shimmering like that thing on my Barclaycard, in a *trouser suit*. It was *not* our usual cashmere-friendly Princess. The *suit* shot great nuclear-powered bolts of light. *Pow pow!* I blinked. 'Hi,' Thing said, in a gravelly voice, advancing across the oatmeal, giving serious retina damage, eye-stabs, a tanned hand volting through the green.

'I'm Lenka.' (Like, 'I'm God.')

The smell! Through my stink-batting blinks, I smelt sandalwood. Rawhide . . . something warm, fetid, like cooked-up blood. *Gross*. Sinead gagged behind her, semaphored slashing her throat. She whispered, loudly, 'Get stinky out!'

I was just about to steer stinky Thingy to the door when—

'What a great', she drawled, reeking, 'evening sky.'

As she turned I caught a glimpse, a shot, of hot red eye. I was plummeting *in* vein.

'I'll just,' she said, simmering, 'lower these blinds.'

And that's when I change. Full DNA. I get furry bleeding expectations. Zebra. Lion. Tiger. Young monkey. I slink up from knackered glamour to skinned-up glamour-puss. *I* could look bleeding great *every* day.

Our fags were burning low.

'I travel,' Lenka said, extracting from her trick lighting a bag of photos, luminous wet jungle scenes, 'and sometimes I import and export . . . you know, well, actually, I make . . .' She smiled/frowned. It was difficult to tell. The air was thickening, joining motes, smooth, dead-red. I was surfing in a kind of ambient trance.

'I make,' Lenka said, '*these.*'

Sinead hit a fur wall. Suddenly, I'm minked, gagging on a fur ball. My hands sunk deep in a snakeskin bra, 38E, my size. Sinead's hands wore, I saw, baby-blue llama shoes, *my* size, like samples, like monkey, tiger, zebra, lemur, like *rare* animals! Like elephant, baboon . . . Like, OK, Protected Species. Well, we ain't vegetarian. My jaw slopped. Spittle pooled on the table like washed-up jewels. Lenka plucked an odd, glittery, desperately backstroking fly out of the air, creamed its blood dot and one crackling rainbow-wing into her skin, slapped down before us, one after the other, tile-sized raw hides, pencil drawings of big, stylish, gorgeous girls with faces, actually, yeah, *exactly* like mine.

'All I want', she said, drawling, 'is to get my head down for a while, somewhere a little anonymous . . . start an exclusive trade, maybe, for Harrods, Harvey Nicks. Maybe make things for,' she mouthed, '*exclusive* folk.'

I looked at Sinead and saw her eyes pop exclusively out on springs.

'I'm not interested', Lenka said, '*necessarily* in being friends.'

It's like we fell from our surfboards. 'Lenka!' we screamed. 'Move in,' we frothed. '*Now!*'

We ran around the house screaming FUUUURRRRR!

*

Insects trailed us like black silk scarves. Crates arrived. A sewing machine. A framed poster of Van Gogh's *Sunflowers*. Lenka: the smell of rawhide, baked blood, a sudden glittery invasion of fruit flies. But, we told each other, *she* is no trouble at all! All we heard, as we whizzed round the house in our big-girls' lingerie, squacking, snorting and spraying Killer Fly, was the background whine of the sewing machine. We hardly saw her. She never went out. She had no friends *whatsoever*, no telephone calls. She cleared up as she went along. She never *ever* left leg hair or tidal waves in the bath. She did get mail though, from funny parts of the world. From the salmon-and-celery-coloured bits. Belting out the door for work, late each day, a fag in my face, I'd tread on her airmail, pale blue and pen-punched like Braille. I'd pass new guys hanging about in the street too, in skinny black suits; kind of jittery, kind of cool; with suntanned indented skulls, like they'd got pulled from the womb, like really long forceps deliveries. Like then

8

they'd got stuck up a pencil sharpener. OK, they weren't into flirting. They'd lean on their long smoky grey cars like they were having their photographs taken. Sometimes, annoyed, me and Sinead we'd go right up to them, right up, and fix our hairstyles and adjust our sarongs in their silverscreen aviator specs. Then Lenka gets, well, she got killed.

\* \* \*

NO CLUES TO MYSTERY WOMAN HIT-AND-RUN, MIDNIGHT
MURDER. LEYTON WOMAN KILLED IN WHITE NIGHTDRESS.
POLICE EXAMINE BLOODY TYRE TRACK.

The moment the service was over me and Sinead went to the pub and sat there really depressed and drank gin. Sinead's navy-blue mascara was smudged but I didn't tell her. We didn't say nothing to each other and didn't talk the next evening after work. Sinead said she'd go and stay at Colin's, her boyfriend's house, as she couldn't stand passing Lenka's door. *She* couldn't stand it. I'd taken Compassionate Leave (well, why not?), so I *had* to be there. Lenka's tights were still hanging up in the bathroom, flapping like peeled bits of fishy skin. So I was on my own and, to say the least, it wasn't very nice. OK, I'll say that sleep was out of the question. Sinead left me all alone in the Palace.

Is that the act of a friend?

I kept hearing creepy noises: sucking and panting, a whine like the sewing machine was still on. It was bleeding Hammer House. The doorbell kept ringing like it rang on its own. I drank five (vertical) fingers of gin for courage and, wearing four pairs of yellow rubber gloves *and* my landlady's hat, off I went into the bathroom, all shivery, and all alone. I got Lenka's debris: her shimmery tights and her hairbrush, with its mat of dead light hair ... down in one and chucked them all in the bin like they're crackling radioactive. Then I *ran* into Lenka's bedroom, intending to whizz round quick with the bin bag. The baked-blood smell hit my nose. The light snapped on. I guess it was the shock or something, the drama, the funeral, all that bleeding gin: I'd *forgotten* about her gear! My hand had a tremble. It flew to my mouth. I saw a black sewing machine in a pearly sheath of dust, one picture beating off the brown wardrobe-coloured wall, Van Gogh's *Sunflowers*, and all this bleeding ... *all this lovely stuff*, strung up on nails, moving like ghost torsos in soft see-through bags. Zebra skirts, lion tights, young monkey— I blinked! There's a whirring noise. I thought, at first, it's my mascaraed eyelashes untangling together. The air filled ... Weird insects, like black crusty helicopters, with crenellated intelligent heads, with wet, tall, blue, fairy-tale wings, broke from the ceiling, whirred briefly around the light bulb. And, plunging, with great plumes of smoke, died.

Picture the wide open O of my mouth.

A mouth couldn't get any O-er.

Wearing EIGHT pairs of yellow rubber gloves I picked the funny crunchy, wingy, leggy bodies up and binned them into the bag. It's lucky I'm not squeamish.

To think! To think I almost didn't *let* Lenka move in.

The stuff was obviously made for *me*. It's a Cinderella fit!

The cuffs fit, the corsets fit, the little sequin A-line rhino-suede skirts rest at the right place along my thigh. In the cupboard I see Lenka's shoe tree.

And reason, she don't need that now, right?

I look in the mirror and, at long last, like I've been searching all sweaty and hot, I see the real cool me.

And back I belt to work.

*

'Hey, girl, welcome back.'

'Eve, I know this sounds just horrible, but grief and trauma *really* suit you.'

'Eve, what *is it* that's different about you?'

*

. . . At night, in my Palace, I dress in Lenka's clothes. I pile my hair up on top of my head, finish my look with her earrings. They're made of herringbone and glass, maybe elbow bone, really strange, kind of luminous. I see them reflected on the blank screen of the telly: them and my sheeny shiny knees . . .

Of course, by the time Sinead gets back, drunk, gin-soaked, bawling (like Lenka and her were like bleeding *best* friends), 'course I'd hidden all the stuff, Lenka's gear, in my room. I replaced it with nylon leopard-skin dresses I get from Walthamstow market: acrylic catsuits, electric-blue fun fur coats. I spray the air with lavender air freshener, buy Killer Fly wholesale. The bleeding Palace is *still* crawling. Wriggly things with big thick brown old-lady legs, with antennae like TV aerials, sprout from the carpet. The air is bugged. My bedroom's turned into a natural history colour slide. Kamikaze insects plop out of some kind of slopped-larva curtain sperm; do one spectacular stunt, like munch air sideways, like beat silver chrome-backed wing mirrors, and die. In the hall outside Lenka's bedroom, I bloody my toes on an outbreak of beetles (with scarlet wide-open jaws, like bottle openers, with split-back hairy wings). Bleeding disgusting. Sinead doesn't see a thing though, cos Sinead's too drunk. I tell Sinead, Lenka was just a crap merchant after all, *not* an exclusive clothes designer. I shake my head at all Lenka's lies. I say, You have this (this nylon shit). Then I say, Sinead, I'm sorry, but your lack of support during this difficult time means we can no longer be friends and I want you out.

Like, 'Sinead,' I say, 'get out now.'

After a stunned half hour, the fake fur flies!

I'm so cool now, I'm cold.

Of course, my friends and Sinead's friends and all our friends in common ring up and come round in queues. I see their silhouettes through the bubble glass of our, *my*, front door, stretching out on the great Leyton skies. What I do though, and this shows such like real bleeding cool, I let my hair go slack and I don't wear make-up, natch, and, as luck would have it, I get a cold sore which eats half my face. I stand in the doorway gibbering like Hamlet, a cloud of flies buzzing round my head, and I look like shit.

'Can you smell,' I ask, desperately sniffing, being like, well, theatrical, 'death?'

'Well,' they say, backing off, 'we sure smell *something*.'

I go all Ophelia and wring my hands. Obviously, I'm breaking down, shattering like a plate of glass, little diamond panes, yeah, diamonds. So, though, at the mo, our friends side with Sinead, I am confident, after a period of transition, they'll side with me. After all, it's not every day a flatmate, someone, granted, you hardly know, gets done, murdered. Hit-and-run. Yeah, it's pretty traumatic.

Who needs friends?

. . . At night, in my Palace, while the phone rings and the door bell goes flat on one note, I blink at the yellow eyes blinking dots throughout my furs. No matter. I turn the central heating dial to nought. Naught seems to live for long. I frown at the mini dragons, stiff as sea horses, tumbling from my sleeves. I flick through my racks, and finally slip into something a little comfy: the petticoat of a lion. In the mirror I re-angle my tortoiseshell pins. Orang-utan slides . . .

And off I belt to work.

*

'Eve, what *is it* that's different about you?'

'Eve, tell us. Are you in love?'

Well, kind of, yeah.

I pile my hair up on top of my head. I look like a million dollars. Million dollars . . . Million dollars . . .

'Eve, what *is it* that's different about you?'

*Moi*? Did I forget to mention this? I am also, if you must know, just really bleeding *rich*.

One night, in the cicada hum of my Palace, call it an instinct, an echo: the spooky gift I inherited off old Mum activates. Like the third finger of my right hand is a divining rod: it sends me vibrating back into Lenka's bedroom. I smell the remnants of her sandalwood perfume. Wild boar. Scabbed blood. My third finger goes into twitch mode when it senses hidden money. Or money in arctic forms. Yeah, my hand trembled near Lenka's framed picture of Van Gogh's *Sunflowers*. I took the picture from the wall; my hand in spasmic blur. Behind the picture was a black velvet gouged-out hole. I thought, at first, like a landlady: cheek *Flippin' cheek!* Inside the gouged-out hole was a crispy dead scorpion, the colour of bruised bad aubergine, and . . . a lucky bag full of . . . diamonds!

It's like my major organs turned to ice cubes. Like I'd swallowed my tongue. Like I'm bleeding *loaded*. I took one diamond and cut through glass. I'm *richhhhhh*!

Come on now, what would you do? Share it with Sinead? Yeah, right on.

At night in my Palace home I take all my clothes off and lie on the oatmeal carpet, like a soft fruit. Naked, I place a line of diamonds along my collar bone, along my ribcage, a couple balanced on my spongy nipples. I pour the rest into my belly button. I feel the carpet under me heave. I get my instamatic Polaroid camera and hold it above my expensive trunk and snap! Now I have someone to celebrate with! I cut my teddy bear open and sew the lucky bag up inside. Good old lucky old ted.

At night I take out the Polaroid of my glittering trunk, hug my ted and smile.

I must not spend conspicuously. I must *not* . . .

I've read enough bad novels (believe me, please) to know I've just got to keep a lid on this. No fast cars. No dashing off to jewellers in Covent Garden. No trips abroad. No ostentatious display. I can tell NO ONE.

The doorbell rings.

Hmm. That's funny. There's no one there. I see the tail end of a smoked-glass car. I look out of my windows and catch a glimpse (or do I? I'm seeing well funny things) of a skinny, shiny, suntanned skull. Like a replay, I think I see the same smoked-glass car cruise across my path, and hear, like footsteps from a parallel world, the flat heavy tread of another's. I spin around just in time to see the edge of a trilby slip inside a door.

Oh, bleeding hell.

I'm like Scarlett O'Hara on this one though. I'll think about it tomorrow.

Or the next day. Or the next day.

The next day I cash in not my diamonds, *my* diamonds, but my savings, my little hard-boiled nest egg of four scraped-up grand. After all, I have new expenses. I go to work by black cab each day, and enjoy the sexual churn, the spin-drying toss of the engine. I casually drop round the corner from our prestigious PR address in the Holloway Road, scattering coins to beggars. I sashay past the slags and slackers. I go to work in my normal uniform of casual PR sexiness: old push-up bra; black. I coo sourly into the phone the same as ever. Although sometimes I cannot resist incorporating some item of Lenka's wardrobe into my gear. Something like a rubber vest, a slashed velvet corset that takes five years off my waist. Stockings with the sheen of retinas. I feel as though my skin has had a chemical peel, revealing the nicer, cuddlier, me. Yes, curious side effect: I *am* nicer. I feel now I can afford to be. I set up two tours for my writers, C&J, which take them right across the country at leisure-break speed. They ring to thank me and, although they do not exactly applaud like seals, they are (suspiciously) pleased.

'Eve, what is that rather unsettling perfume?'

Money, girl. Money smells. And I smell? Bleeding *great*!

*

And where can a single girl have a great time out in London, in full apparel? Gay bars.

In the gay bars, thanks to Lenka's wardrobe, I'm soon surrounded and I have one great time. Boys want to try on my clothes. They want to stroke along my arms. They are interested in the texture of me: zebra, lion, young monkey. No no, I demur. These are expensive imitations. I'm a Vegan myself. Home in a black cab, a pretty boy limp across my lap (I feel his fingers try to ease off my buckskin shoes), a ring of cocaine round my nostrils, inside my nose flap two pretty, mini, ermine furs.

*

My luck runs. It's on a gallop. I watch the Leyton skies turn into beaten gold plate. Luck breeds luck. I win a scratch-card lottery: five hundred grand. The newsagent goes berserk! I get my photo taken with his entire family grinning ear to ear. I bless this lucky newsagent's. I publicly accept the giant cheque, donate a couple of grand to a donkey charity and, in a spirit of largesse, write a cheque out to Sinead. It comes back like confetti. There's a note. The note reads—

Well. No matter. I won't think about that today. Lenka's clothes can come out to play.

I can look *bleeding great* every day. These, I say, oh, these are *très-très-très* expensive imitations. I get them from the most darling secret little shop.

Though I notice they're not fitting *quite* as well. I look a little ashen, a little, maybe, sick around the gills. Underneath my eyes are two tiny pale-blue Prada bags. There's a buzzing in my ears as though my head is full of flies.

I slip my key into my Palace door and hear, for a moment, the shrill roar of a forest floor. Cicadas. Timballing. I walk across my Axminster and feel, through my heels, crunch . . . crunch . . .

. . . I lie on the couch. Insects sprout and die around me. Ants and beetles lock horns. Termites leave their umbrellas empty. I lose my appetite for the gay bars of London. For an anodyne flirt I flick through a pile of travel brochures, but I don't quite feel up to Peru, New Mexico, New York, New York. And, as I try on a mini dress made from glossy blue spider skins, knitted spider legs, or a cape made from the combined stomach linings of armadillos and beaver cubs, the walls of my Palace dissolve, and I see, with full throat, me and Sinead sitting out on the front steps in our old big bikinis, our leaf-dappled sarongs. I see me and Sinead planting plastic orchids in Derek's back garden. Or moving the magnetic sheep on the fridge rota. Or throwing suitcases into the street.

Lorries roar by like trains. I try to recreate the soundtrack of our jokes . . . *Just a spot of late night welding, girls* . . . and fail. At night, at 4 a.m., what I count, anyway, as night, I find I'm up on my uppers. I wake each time in Lenka's bedroom, my hand on the freezing curve of her sewing machine, my hand imprinted on the pearly dust. The clear plastic bags shrink up on the nails like husks. The air breathes bad. Of bad meat. There's a buzzing sound. And I don't recall . . . I don't recall those blackcurrant curtains. From the top of the stairs, through the bubble glass of the front door, I think I glimpse the shiny skid of a skull. Through the bubble glass of the front door I think I see the thick blue beard growth of the baddy.

Will I one night, in a trance, wearing a vampire victim's white lace nightie, showing my crayoned-on veins, my erect stick-on nipples, lift up the latch and let him in? I see the blood stains of Leyton sky behind him.

But this ain't a story with a bleedy ending like that.

In the roar of my Palace I'm sitting here resting up, real pretty, real rich.

# *Shop Talk*

She was pulling out Hoover coils. 'Well, he just goes into a moody so I think . . .'

'I'm not joking, his eyes bored into me like that snake in *The Jungle Book*.'

'In the back of the shop the click of the kettle, coffee clouds, the gold crusts of microwaved croissants. Quarter of an hour before the soundtrack reeled on. Sal drew on a wide purple mouth.

'What did you do last night, Sal?'

'TV. Dinner. Bed.' Fight.

\*

Loll's armchair. Her couch.

In the bathroom her toiletries on two packed shelves, some of them gluey and furred with dust. Some of them laced together with cobweb. He saw a spider strung between a Vosene bottle and an exfoliating skin cream, short, iron trapezing legs. His toothbrush and electric shaver. His toothbrush and electric shaver took up four square centimetres. 'Four square centimetres.'

'If you're measuring I'd make that two,' she leered.

He laughed. But thought: You bitch.

And took that thought to work.

And crushed it with a spanner, under a Nissan's dark low troubled sky. Twisted it round a nut. 'And suddenly, she's wearing *pan*da slippers.' He rolled out on his back, looked up through the sheen of navy-blue covered yard, at Steve in his goggles, flame-throwing wrecks. The silhouettes of his springy mustard-cress hair. 'What'ja think, Steve?'

Steve said, 'Chuck her.'

\*

'That really suits you.' Sal ran the back of a hand down the rack of Ghost, Nicole Farhi, French Connection, Sturgeon, the corral of alarm-rich black leather shirts. All day she galloped round in faux fur boots, tilting like a pretty sea horse, whacked by texture, colour, sounds. By four o'clock, shaking with caffeine, they all went really, *really* mad to Gypsy Kings, running in and out of the changing rooms, plaiting their hands in front of their faces like four Björks. She loved working here. Dressing up as a different woman every day.

She wrote lyrics on the back of paper bags. She sounded so great in her pink soapy bath. Hair piled up like a sparkly cone of vanilla ice cream.

\*

'I've always loved, don't know why,' Steve said, holding up a flaking orange socket spanner, 'short, you know, fat girls.'

\*

'Mmm,' said the customer, wriggling down a pink sausage skin, 'do you think it makes my bum look too wide?'

Yes, Sal thought. 'No. It *really* suits you . . . That'll be four hundred and seventy-five pounds.'

'That'll be a month's mortgage and a trip to Safeway's.'

'Bye now, don't forget your receipt.'

She had to swallow hard sometimes. Tongue dry. Like she was going to cry. She wrote on a gold-sprayed paper bag: 'Surrounded by plenty baby, baby, tears in my throat, la la la.'

'He came in, right, said he'd like to try it on as he happened to be *exactly* the same size as his wife. Looked straight at me. I looked *straight* back.'

'What you doing tonight, Sal?'

'Dinner. Video. Pub.' Fight.

She saw Loll on his armchair, scowling.

*

Steve said, 'Wear two condoms from now on. Once it gets domestic . . .'

Domestic. It rang in his head.

'Once she, she washed my overalls, right. Couldn't *stand* that. Like she'd f-fing wiped me out . . .' Years of wiping oil and brown grease on his thighs so they caked, each day like slipping pale fuzzy legs through a map of himself. Saw his overalls sloshing up against the glass bright blue. 'I don't f-fing *believe it.*'

'I couldn't get this *particular* stain out, Loll.' She'd said, pointing out one left. From a Laguna he'd skinned down in January '92.

He'd had to sit back on the couch like he'd been whacked.

He'd go home and clear her the hell out. Her three wardrobes and ten shelves. His one chrome bar. Her . . .

\*

'. . . Love me baby, aha aha, as I am . . .'

'Tofu? It's like thigh fat that tofu stuff, innit. Like eating someone else's cellulite.'

\*

He fiddled in the innards of a crushed silver Golf GTI, eyes half shuttered like a vet's, moving his oiled and corded forearm round like he was easing a calf out: slipping it through two wet clenched cow walls. He blinked through the subterranean gloom, through the scorched plastic double take of his goggles, saw, with a grin, Steve skim the stained ocean floor. 'Yo. *Yo!*' In the gates, in a pale lozenge of yellow sunshine, two chubby schoolgirls clicked past. Steve cooing lewd, 'Babies. Yo there, baby dolls.'

Loll grinning, shaking his head like a suede dog.

\*

'I'm not joking, I read about it in a book. It's a test. You throw them . . .' she whispered, '*your knickers*, like pasta, up against the wall.' She rang up the till, threw in a bag a parachute of silk. 'If they stick, you fancy him. If they don't, well, you're just drunk.'

A mauve Donna Karan sheath dress sheathed in plastic near the till. £595. She touched it all day, reverently slipped her hand in for its cool inside, the frisson it gave her silk palm, sending her reeling out with the lunch list from throbbing Seal into the blowy silent-by-comparison high street. Feeling a kind of pleasant anguish as though someone were about to lift up her hair, shiver-kiss her neck. The chill of the fruit counter in M&S, holding four tuna fish with mayo on brown; apricots, a lemon fruit spritzer they'd drink in champagne glasses for lunch.

\*

A hush round it. Spotlit in the centre of the yard. Seagull doors. Glassed-in lights. Walnut panelling. Expensive perforated tack. He slid inside the lilac upholstery, breathed in turtle wax, the intimate scent of new car: one expensive – from the stub in the ashtray – briefly smoked cigar. He pulled on the wristy gears. Grunt from the engine. Brand new and the fucker wouldn't start. Palmed his groin down hard. Pushed in an ancient CD. Madness. 'One Step Beyond'. Pushed his head through the sun roof mouthing, 'ONE STEP BE-YOND.' Had a dance about before lunch, stamping boots through petrol-coloured puddles. Felt joy briefly kick in. And kick out. Slumped over his pineapple juice in the pub.

'Eat up,' Steve said, eating, mash on his tongue.

'Can't. Full up.'

\*

'They videoed the birth.'

'No!'

'Yes! Video *nasty*! When she tore you could hear it on the Sony. Like, have you ever ripped rotten sheets really quickly?'

\*

'*Fuck!*' A piss-spurt from an oil tank blacked his eye. Laughing. Their laughter ran up like rodents and bellowed off the tiles. Listening, head back, to the last echo notes, he heard Sal squeech away in the bath. And felt for her a little, leaky, belly-ache of warmth.

\*

'Should babies wear make-up?'
  'No, if they're ugly. No. Like – *that one last week, urgh!*'
  They stood in the corner, gagging, panting after a Gypsy Kings workout. She looked at them, at their white leather sheaths, brightly coloured hair. She must look just like them. Shop girls. Mutant fruits. A quick feeling of revolt. A revolting feeling.
  'Fruit sisters, yeah, we are fruit . . .'
  End of day. Setting the alarm. Keying in her birth date and half of Loll's. Something de-tagged, rolled up tight beneath her arm.

\*

Day over. Locking the garage door with Steve, a quick game of noughts and crosses in the dotty grime between thick, blackly oiled crossbars. He won. Walking, loosened, home.
  'Nice day, Sal?'
  She was cutting up a pineapple on the crowded kitchen

table, her back to him, shaped like an egg-timer in a new mauve dress. 'Yeah, not bad. Yours?'

He quickly assessed. 'Yeah, 'bout 'same. Hey, Sally girl.' She turned round. 'You're looking . . . er, well, good.' He grinned. 'Why don't you, um . . . get over here?'

*Plastered*

My name's Tony Wornel, to cut a long story short. I believe in acting on first impressions, so when I see a bird at a party I go up to them, find their best feature and say, 'Great hair,' or, 'Hey,' pointing, *cat's* eyes.' It works one time out of ten. That's not a bad average. When I say 'works' I mean social not sexual intercourse. I don't believe in using birds like that. I like a chat. I subscribe to a number of interesting magazines. I've got a stack of magazine knowledge inside me and, as I work in market research, I'm really good at moving the knowledge round. After a good night out, if I've scored my one in ten, got a little *parlez-vous* going, when I get back home I feel really full of the possible. Even if it's been raining or even snowing, even if the backdrop is like depressing. I get back home and bound upstairs to my bed and think about what a *great* evening I've had.

Katy, to cut a long story short, really did have 'great hair'. It was up around her like a halo, almost like an Afro, but kind of wheat coloured. It was her who started me off on my interior design. Like, time to sort out my spiritual home. Like I had to clear out, then decorate a really dark place. Like a cellar or a crypt.

My name, as I've said, is Tony Wornel, and I'm thirty-two

years old and I've just left home. I mean my parent's home, Mr and Mrs Wornel. I still lived at home as it was cheap: I got my cleaning done, my clothes ironed and my food on time. Renting's a mug's game. I lived right up by Manor House station so it was straight down the Piccadilly Line in the mornings. No messing. My bedroom was more of a bachelor pad. Like a spread. Well, I could afford it. I had a mirror on the back door so I could see myself lying back on my big chrome bed. It's like all my exteriors were sorted: leather, pin lighting, black carpet, chrome. Built-in wardrobes so it was all strictly minimalist. Like I say, I'm good with information. I've got the top-quality range of electrical equipment and my own phone. If the phone rings I'm always playing jazz. Count Basie. You know, shit like that.

Renting really *is* a mug's game. This bedsit is now more of a lock-up: my gear's all squashed in and looks a bit stupid. Now I'm almost hoping, what with the mega insurance premiums, the whole lot gets nicked.

I could bring birds back home as well if I wanted.

My parents weren't bothered. They'd watch TV all night like switched-off robots with human eyes. They'd only switch on again if Helen – God Almighty – my twin sister rang up from Australia.

Me, I like to keep busy. I like to play hard. In the evenings, if I'm not out partying, then I'm reading through my mags, or playing my electric guitar or my jazz CDs. I've got a Complete Jazz Lover's Collection from the *Sunday Times Magazine* (though I'd say jazz is more a taste I'm acquiring). What I'd really like is to play in a rock band, as a hobby. Hence the electric guitar. I can strum it a bit but, really, I can't play it standing up yet, and rock bands won't exactly provide chairs. I've got to get that sorted. Gigs are great venues for chatting up birds. You can see all the good ones from the stage. The ones up for it, for a chat.

I meet a lot of birds at work with 'great eyes', 'clear handwriting', 'nice handbags', but, because market research is such a cut-throat business, there's never any time for a good old chat. Since my accident though, they've been all over me like a rash. There's a gang at work known as the Marketeers, and they're really tight. They form an even tighter circle later on in the pub. At work, at Research Services Ltd, they don't notice the real me because of my persona. I'm like Squirrel Man, squirrelling away at my information. My job is to pump information into the computer *as* the gang are handing in their clipboards. It's pressurized stuff. Their job is quite pressurized as well – what with having to stop tetchy people on the streets and at airports. It's one of those work hard, play hard places. I'm quick. I'm efficient. And people only notice if you make a mess. They don't know that old Tony Wornel becomes Tone the minute he gets back home and takes off his office jacket and puts on his leathers. They don't know that I sleep in black satin sheets and play electric guitar or that sometimes I lie back on my big chrome bed and feel really full of the possible.

The time I met Katy was quite a highlight and started me tripping into my interior, which, as I've said, is actually quite a dark place. Like I thought, It's about time I got that sorted. Like properly lit. As I said, I'm thirty-two years old. I like to play hard. I like to go on first impressions and go with the flow. I like to augment my magazine knowledge with personal experience. Some of my evenings out can be like adventures. To cut a long story short, the night of my accident was one such. I mean adventure. It was raining first off, which was annoying as I'd only Mum's poxy new polka-dot umbrella (which is shaped like a parasol and has the radius of a saucer and if my hair gets wet it goes fluffy and horrible, and also a bit bald looking). I was in the Coach and Horses first for a few pints, peaked a bit too early, and then off I went to this party on the Amhurst Road. I just followed these three birds holding a couple of cans. In this party, though, it was like *all* black birds and me. They looked at me really funny and that might have been because I'm like white, and it might have been because I'm like a white bloke, and it might have been that I didn't actually bring any drink and was pretty tanked up already and still, unfortunately, holding the parasol umbrella. '*Great* party,' I said, just as the music went quiet.

I've read somewhere, in a magazine, that if friendliness fails (which it did), acting a bit berserk in a potentially dangerous situation can act as a protective shield. So I started dancing a bit, like Mary Poppins on E, thrashing around, and, when I came to, I was outside on the pavement, kind of down on my nose. For a long time. And I hurt all over. I felt a tug at my shoulder and a voice saying, 'Oh, leave him, Katy, he's drunk.' I rolled over, groaning. I looked up and I saw it. *Great* hair.

'My name,' I mouthed, 'is Tony Wornel.'

To cut a long story short, that's how I met Katy and Tracy:

a sweet bird and a sour one. They took me back to their flat on the Amhurst Road. I was screaming, 'I'm *Tony Wornel*,' don't ask me why. The whole empty road was spinning like a spin-dryer. I had concussion. The parked cars and the shining brown pavement was sky one minute, and the stars were like under my feet making a horrible crunchy noise the next. Then the stars were exploding like fireworks. That was great. Katy and Tracy lived about five flights up, no lift, which wasn't so great. I had an arm round both of them. They had to practically carry me. This Katy one was really soothing. It turned out they're both like – *nurses*! ICN! My luck! When I come round I'm in Patient Heaven, feeling no pain, floating on a couch covered by scarfs and like girly junk (like pots of blue nail polish digging in my back), and these two nurses were like intensively caring for me, daubing me with red *essence de hospital*. It was like feminine and cosy in the flat. The whole place was asway with plant tendrils and smelt of pasta and like hot wine. The carpet had giant jigsaw puzzle outlines on it and a game of Monopoly full of housing estates. It looked lived in. And, though it was feminine, and I like, as I've said, manly-minimalist, I felt right at home. Lying there, at the centre of it all, as it were, I get full of the possible. I thought, if *my* interior was a room, then this is the kind of room it should be. What a great evening! I get a revelation. I spend the whole night on the couch. I get to sleep with two birds. Tracy, the sour one, said she's not going to bed while 'he's here', so they both had to sit up all night nodding off in their armchairs like proper night nurses. I did directional moaning each time I saw Katy nod off in particular. She was great awake, really caring: doing the whole business: feeling my pulse, taking my temperature, the works. In the morning, my luck held out because, actually, I did have a cracked femur and I had to go to hospital. It was really great all going to work, as it were, together.

To cut a long story short, the moment I got that plaster of Paris on my leg, well, it was brilliant. It was like all I'd needed was that extra bit of support. A prop. What a sea change at work! When the birds clocked me on my crutches limping along in this snowy white knee-length plaster, immediately they're all dead nice to me and want to write on my cast. They even make me a get well card. Get Well Tony Wornel, except they spell my name wrong. Thereafter, when I get to parties, instead of me having to do all the describing – 'Great hair', 'Lovely teeth', 'Coloured contact lenses, *surely*?' – birds more or less come up to me. I guess it's because I look so vulnerable leaning forward on my crutches. Personal injury is a great conversational gambit. Even on the Piccadilly Line. Instead of me saying, I got the shit kicked out of me for gatecrashing this party, or like, These birds beat me up, I say, I did it skiing, or, There was a fire at home and I had to jump out of the first floor window holding my baby brother. It's brilliant. I get to shift quite a lot of my magazine knowledge. I get just great social intercourse. And the backdrop, as it were, comes forward.

*

In the mornings the sun was really bright. The birds sang. I mean, instead of the usual dense racket, I was hearing tunes.

All the privet hedges shone and the tops of cars and even the puddles outside the station glinted kind of merrily. Midges danced about in the air. When I pulled my blinds up in the morning I felt like I was pulling up two extra eyelids.

Of course I went back to Katy and Tracy's flat a number of times to thank them for their many kindnesses. I got their phone number as well. The first time I brought nothing too fancy, something fairly understated: a bunch of blue corn-flowers to match Katy's eyes and a box of after dinner (hint hint) mints. They couldn't let me in though, as they were just about to go on shift. The next time I got to sit on the couch, right at their centre, as it were, for a while, and just chat and chat away, and Tracy even went out and left me alone with Katy, who I much preferred of course anyway. Unfortunately, the phone rang about then and Katy had to rush back to hospital due to an emergency situation. Nurses *really* work hard.

At work, at Research Services Ltd, well, it was all great. Once a week I cleaned the graffiti off my plaster of Paris with Tippex and shoe whitener so it was like brand new and just cried out to be scribbled on. Some of the birds were really extra nice to me so there was plenty to think about when I got home and lay on my bed listening to my jazz CDs. When my leg plaster was clean it became like the Office Notice Board. Birds wrote things like: GARY KIBLIN IS A TWIT. Gary would come along, kind of sarcastically, in his big black baggy suit, and cross out the t. Quite a crowd gathered round me sometimes, all scribbling and laughing away while I punched in the front-line information: MR HARRISON HAS GOT

GINGER PUBES; MICHELLE COWLEY IS A COW. They're a great crowd at work. Even when I went to the pub, room was always made for me and my crutches. It was like I was sat at the centre of a wonderful dream.

At night, I slept in a velvet pit, all smiles while my leg had a hug in its cast. The clean lines of my crutches really pleased me up against my white wood-chipped walls, really added to my exterior, and, when I was out playing really hard somewhere, I leaned on the snug black leather cushions tucked under my arms like I was leaning into more of me. They proved quite useful as well. Sometimes, after some hard play, I'd be drawn up to Katy and Tracy's flat, especially after a couple of pints, and that's when the combination of heavy plaster, two crutches and two essentially caring nurses paid off. As the flat is five flights up, by the time I'd slogged up there I'd usually be covered, dripping, actually, in sweat, and if Katy and Tracy were in (which they were as I'd see them get home), then, well, they could hardly turn me away on my crutches. I felt really close to Katy especially, like she was my spiritual twin, like we'd got separated at birth, and what I found I wanted more than anything else, was to lie straight down on that couch again. Like, get in touch with my centre, be intensively cared for once more. One night it was pretty great there because I got to eat pizza with them and watch a video. Tracy even called me a taxi. At the door I told her she has 'great eyes', even though she's got eyes like pins. Birds love a random compliment.

Unfortunately, my hospital appointment to have my plaster taken off threatened to cut off my dream. In the morning

Mum kept giving me the white appointment card as I hopped off to work. I was looking forward to having that plaster removed like I'd look forward to having a head amputation. Mum kept going on about it. I missed the first appointment accidentally on purpose, and it got deferred for a week. Then I missed that one as well.

Eventually, Mum calls the doctor round to the house herself. Apart from her being annoyed with me for clumping about on the ceiling, the hospital really want those crutches back and keep phoning up. I tell the doctor I'm prepared to buy them off him myself, like pay, I whisper, cash, but he wasn't having any of that. In fact he went into a bit of a rant about chipping and cutting at the NHS, about bloody users/ sponges/leeches/time-wasters, the usual stuff, but, as he was holding this spinning wheel drill thing over my leg at the time, it all got a bit scary. To calm him down I tell him he's got 'healing hands'. Compliments don't really work on blokes. He broke the plaster in front of me, which was annoying as I was actually planning to re-use it again.

The sight of my leg after the plaster came off was horrible, quite a shock. Compared with the other one, it was all withered and scaly. Mum said it reminded her of me next to Helen in the incubator. When I scratched it, my skin flaked off. It was horrible. It was like my black carpet had dandruff. I oiled the leg down and then, brainwave, as it felt quite fragile, I wound bandages around it all the way past my ankle. I even rolled my suit trousers up a bit so it got noticed at work. That was OK for the first couple of days, but then all the little attentions I got from having the plaster on in the first place wore off. At the coffee percolator it was strictly Pour the Coffee and Go. The Marketeers, well, when I approached their circle in the pub, that seat or this seat was always taken, so it got a bit tough-going standing up at the bar.

At home, well, to cut a long story short, it was like the long autumn and winter of my discontent. The backdrop really got to me. If it wasn't snowing it was raining kind of thick mud. I had one fluffy-hair day after another. I lay on my bed listening to my jazz CDs, but actually, without the weight of the plaster, I began to feel a bit light-headed, like the notes were like worms in my eardrums, making me feel quite nauseous. Dizzy and annoyed. Jazz is quite a discordant noise. I don't think I really like it that much. My leg throbbed as well. I wrapped the bandages even tighter but it still kind of bleated. At work I got noticed for making a mess and got called to head office twice. Yelled at. That Gary Kiblin kept leaping on to my desk, flapping his black suit jacket over his head like wings, like he was a vulture and I was the dead stinking bit of meat already. At home, I lay on my bed and played my electric guitar or played jazz really loudly just in case Katy and Tracy rang. They didn't. Mum and Dad banged on the ceiling and Dad came in a couple of times and took all my plugs.

I got to go to a couple of parties after that, but I think, around then, I must have caught post-viral/broken leg syndrome or something. It was quite an effort standing in the hall at parties. For a while I got off on 'Great dress', and, when the bird started thinking perhaps that was too personal a comment, like too close to her precious naked skin, I'd say, 'My girlfriend's got one the exact same.' Or I'd whisper, at super-emergency compliment time, 'It suits you much better.'

I got myself up to Katy and Tracy's flat quite a few more times, against quite a depressing backdrop of slurpy snow. If Tracy, Nurse Ratchet-Features, opened the door though, well, it's like I'd get to see her and the inside of the flat for about one second. That bird could turn sugar sour, whole hay lofts full of apples, cure diabetes. I'd hate to be her patient. She's got fat arms as well. 'Nice jumper,' I said, just as the door slammed.

If Katy answered though, well, she's a bit of a soft touch – especially as I often had a fluffy toy or something, a flower behind my back. She'd jump a bit with surprise. A couple of times I got to sit with her while she made herself ready for work. I'd see her in her nurse's uniform, but actually, I don't know why people go on about them being sexy or something, because actually they're like blue sacks. Katy, if anything, got more business-like in her uniform. Quite abrupt and bossy. She went on about how hard nursing is, how they need time to unwind, as if I don't. Like my job's easy. I switched off a bit while her mouth worked. Her hair though, above the bland uniform, was really great to look at. Haloed. When I was back in my bed I'd dream I was brushing it, or I was a tiny thing lying in it, like a flea or a kirby grip really gripping in tight.

\*

Well, to cut a long story short, it turned out Mum and Dad had been planning to emigrate to Australia for quite some time. They sprang this news on me suddenly. They weren't planning on taking me with them either. Ms God Almighty, Helen, was on the phone braying day and night and vice-versa. One day I came home from work and found a red FOR SALE sign in our front garden. A month later a SOLD sign was slapped over that. Suddenly, I'm in a robot clearing hall. Crates were packed. Lists made, ticked and crossed off. Mum and Dad were really humanoid, fully switched on. I was going to be homeless. I had to keep mouthing that to myself to make it true. *My name is Tony Wornel and I am going to be homeless*. Then, it *was* true. I waved my parents off at Heathrow and off they flew, away. I only had a couple of weeks to find somewhere else to live. At work, it was back to my squirrelling days. Tony Wornel punching in his infor-mation. I really wanted to get lifted out of myself. Be Tone out partying, having a chat. I tied my support bandages on really tight and let the pavement convey me whither. I was trying to stay really open to the possible.

One night I followed these two birds holding a bottle of wine into a house, and that's how I got the black eye. Unfortunately, that was on a Friday night. By Monday morn-ing it was gone completely so nobody could make a fuss at work, or like get me a card.

It was quiet in the house. Not nice 'n' quiet. More like a water torture noise in a tomb. When I couldn't bear that kind of quiet any more I pressed the redial button on my fax–phone. Katy and Tracy rarely answered it. Then an answerphone answered, and after the bleep I found myself suspended right above the possible. I heard all this static in my ear. Like the static was *inside* me. Crackling. Like I was listening to an echo of my interior. Quite frightening. Then I realized it was just me breathing.

Each night I'd take a long short cut home from work and sit outside Katy and Tracy's flat re-winding the bandages on my leg. I was hoping Katy and Tracy would see me and come down and help, or, better yet, invite me up to their flat for a chat. Their window looked really steamed-up and cosy, full of warm yellow light. I imagined they were eating pepperoni pizza and walking around in their half slips, smoking French fags, and arguing about whose hotels were on New Bond Street. I was supposed to be out looking for a bedsit. Then I got this bedsit on Downs Park Road (no view of the downs though) and, without much ado, well, none, I moved in. As I said, my chrome and black leather looks pretty stupid in here. The walls *and* the ceiling have been papered, more like peppered over, with poppy wallpaper. Waking up in the mornings the poppies look like bloody, messy bullet holes.

I've decided to sell all my electric wizardry before some bastard nicks it.

One night I knocked on Katy and Tracy's door after I'd drunk a few too many in the Bar Lorca. I got really depressed in the Bar Lorca. I couldn't work on my conversational gambits as the music was too loud and it was that Latin stuff that worries away at your solar plexus. At the bar it was like I was speaking an underwater language or something and this Irish bird kept laughing at everything I said. And these couples were spinning around making me feel sick. Anyway, I managed to get into Katy and Tracy's flat by crying, and at first I'm really putting it on so I can get to sit on that couch and get looked after, but then I really *am* crying. I peeped through my fingers and explained (lying a bit) I was going to be homeless soon and could I stay on their couch. I saw Katy falter but that bitch Tracy was in there straight away. Quite rude as well, the fat cunt. She practically got me by the collar and threw me out. 'Nice shoes,' I managed, as the door slammed.

Anyway, to cut a long story short, last night I got up there again. I'd already tripped up on the pavement as my support bandage had come undone, so my nose was bleeding. I didn't clear the mess up though, as I thought it might reactivate Katy's slack caring hormones. Tracy was at work. (I'd made sure of that.) I'd bought a new chrome suitcase. I thought, If I could just get my tartan toothbrush in between theirs, I could get my exteriors sorted again. I'm good with exteriors. I should have just stuck with that. And I thought how great it would be living with two birds. Like midnight chats. Like videos and guitar-playing and reading magazine knowledge out loud. I was having those kinds of fantasies when Katy opened the door. Her bottom lip went all quivery when she saw me. Quite emotional. She really did look like an angel. The hall light was shining through her frizzy hair. She looked quite celestial. I stated my case, so to speak. I got my foot through the door, sniffing back a large black blood bubble, when suddenly there's this big bloke standing in front of me. He says, 'I'll handle him, Kate.' I say, 'Whoa, great muscles, do you work o—'

## Plastered

Compliments don't really work on blokes. When I wake up I'm in a hospital ward but I'm feeling no pain. This nurse tells me I'll have to wear this neck brace for about six months. *And* I've busted my femur bone again. Well, I couldn't be happier. I'm really feeling full of the possible. 'Mantula,' I say, reading this nurse-bird's name tag, passing into Unconscious Land. 'Hey, *un*usual name.'

*Tell Her You Love Her*

When he was very young they all chased after him, in kiss chase gangs, pushed their lips on him, pushed their desks near him, walked him home from school, sent him padded scarlet hearts: BE MY VALENTINE. Like a cartoon boy he was quick to blush. Then, he expected love. There he is, centre-back in photographs: pretty baby heart-breaker.

Women all the time, through the alphabet, then in single sullen file, all the way from A: Angie, Angeline, Betty, Bettine . . . Kay, Janine . . . and so on. Till he stuck with M. Stuck with Monica.

That girl's stuck to you, Ron said, like superglue. You should do yourself a favour, Kyle. Tell her you love her.

I don't.

You're missing me point, Ron's Guinness moustache twirled. Do *yourself* a favour.

In the nook, through the smoky after-hours gloom, Ron's yellow eyes glowed out like an Alsation dog's. Tell her you love her. She'll blossom like a flower.

Kyle said, That's what flowers do, flower, flower. They also, Ron said, rot.

Monica swayed towards them in her hippy A-line skirt, slopping three pints, her bottom lip ledged out. Ron said, The girl looks peeved. Simulate to stimulate mate, little things. He winked towards the fruit machines, yanked down arms. I'll leave you two to coo. Monica said, I . . . hate him. Why does he have to come out with us ALL THE TIME? They heard the distinct cascade of Ron's win. Kyle leant across the table. He touched Monica's skin. She flinched. Under his warm finger-probe her cheek was oily, bunched. Then, bumped like sand . . . paper. Porous, like a close-up of a desert. He swallowed visibly, trailed away as though greatly moved: You look . . .

Monica clutched her pint, confused.

At the Sunday kick-around, Ron said, every so often, Touch her, above the elbow, on her throat, like you're checking her, you know, fucking pulse. He kicked the squashy ball up through the bleached winter air. A roar from the sidelines. Ron's beautiful wife, his four beautiful kids clapped their hands.

Further back, on a muddy black path, in a Fiat, through a patch of steam, Ron's beautiful girlfriend, Sesame, mimed delight.

Think of her, Ron said, lining up a snooker cue, like a . . . pension plan. You know you've got to have one.

If you died, Ron said, I'd come to the funeral. I'd bring the wife but, let's face it, who else would come? Thank you very much, said Kyle. Ron said, You're stuck with her. Why be miserable? You could shine her up like varnish.

*

Kyle repped shops. He broke hearts. His smile clung to the warm carpet-smelling bookshop air. His feet crunched hearts. Of late, a burn in his guts, a nauseous slide. The start of a peptic ulcer? It felt slightly better when he ate.

He ate. He felt slightly better when he ate.

He picked Monica up after work, outside the Pizza Express. He came at her from the snow shadows, through a flurry of cold wet flakes. Mmm, come here, He found, of late, he liked meeting her straight from work. She came towards him smelling of meals, of celery and fresh fag smoke. He traced her hip bone through her coat, through her tight work skirt, worried a firm wormy vein there. In these clothes, a brilliantly red lipstick, she looked not hippy but hip. She said, What's going on Kyle?

In his flat, Kyle picked up a glass. His fingers were tingling. The glass felt odd in his hands. Heavy and light, as though he could feel the molecules in their constant whizzing flight. He saw the smear of her work red lipstick.

In the bath, his erection splashed up through the grey and green suds. He looked into its one squint eye as though he looked straight at someone else.

Ron said, in the betting shop, screwing his face down over the minute yellow pads, Don't tell her yet, you've got to like ... *excruciate* them. His dog-face zoomed in on the TV screen. One hand urged on his thigh. YES! Fifty smackaroonies. My advice is ...

In her flat, Monica sat on the couch damply wrapped after a hot bath. She sipped her nightly joint and watched TV.

She'd told her flatmate, I think Kyle's taking the piss out of me. Her flat mate said, Kyle does take the piss out of you. The phone rang. It was Kyle. Hi, he said. His breath came out of the handset like a warm spicy breeze. Just ringing up to say goodnight. Goodnight, Monica said, and slammed the phone down.

Kyle looked in the mirror. His razor cut furrows through the snow on his jaw. His pretty face gazed seriously back, skin gathered up on his brow in a loose question mark. He'd had a peculiar dream. In his dream Monica stood upon a giant oyster shell, shyly cupping her breasts, her lank hair, in Dream Land, dreamily long. He pleaded with her through a cone megaphone, Please Monica.

His please all z's and e's. Monica pleeezeeeze!

He felt a kind of vertiginous horror.

And didn't ring her for two days. He put his answerphone on and cooked through her calls.

He zoomed up and down the purple pre-spring motorways, under the spume of lorries, ferrying his sackful of samples, free T-shirts, free smiles and books till the dream went away.

He dreamt instead of a scarlet inflating heart.

At the cinema, in the grainy dark, Kyle kissed Monica just above the eye. His tongue flicked delicately at the edge of her spiky eyebrow. He cupped her breasts through the cups of her scratchy white bra. You are a Martian, Monica whispered. What have you done with Kyle? I think there must be a pod in your basement.

Spring. Pale-green watery air. On impulse he bought Monica a bunch of flowers from a windswept motorway stall.

The flowers were fussy in silver tinsel paper, the petals over-bright, as though a child had, enthusiastically, tongue out, felt-tipped the colour in. He saw her face break. Now she knew he was joking. She placed the ugly flowers in the sink and ran the tap over them. He watched the colour flood out.

He bought her white lilies next time. She centred them on the dining room table, in a tall clear vase. The flowers were so fresh he could almost hear them drink. They quivered with the music pumping out of her stereo. In the late afternoon they gathered in all the light, grew still and luminously green like a set of startled brides. He found himself approaching them sideways, peering, weirdly aroused, up into their rustling flute-shaped skirts.

*

Time to make love, Ron said. He said 'lurve'. He bounced Sesame on his knee on the tartan picnic blanket. On the damp summer grass a champagne bottle crackled, sank in a melting bag of ice. Make lurve to me, my Sesame. Ron looked over her plaited tresses, puckered his lips at Kyle. Time, he said, to stroke.

Don't tell me how to fucking fuck, said Kyle.

In his car, at the edge of the park, Kyle sat shaking with the motor running, his head lowering into the dashboard, as though expecting the white bashing bloom of an air bag.

In bed with Monica he stroked her slowly and kissed her feet. Her toes smelt faintly, though not unpleasantly, of plimsolls, a sweet violet talcum powdered sweat. He smelt playgrounds. She squealed. But he was serious, quiet. He stroked her badly shaved legs, a friction built up under his palms. Her limbs grew heavy, then heavier, as though they filled slowly with dark blue water, or, he couldn't decide, a dark blue pushing air. Her face, when he found it, was astonishingly bright. She said, What did you say? Words tumbled out. He felt their ricochet. They crashed up into his chest, exploded like dry dusty rocks. He saw, for a moment, superimposed on hers, Ron's laughing cracked-up face. He collapsed boneless, fell through her damp splayed hair. The yield of the pillow. She must have felt his blush heat. Oh, she said. Then, very slowly, Oh, dear.

# Enquiries (General)

As I work for a well-known building society as a receptionist – Enquiries (General) – and, to say the least, I'm well above average looking, some people assume, before they know the real me, that I am thick. However, I am not. I am not on Enquiries (General) because I can't add up – this is what the other girls, Tracy and Emelda, say – but because I have a *generally enquiring mind*. For instance, if a client (we never say customer in this building society) were to ask, 'Nicola, what inhabitant of rivers and lakes plays host to the bilharzia worm?' I would naturally say, 'The snail.' Similarly, if another client were to ask, 'What book is subtitled *The Preservation of Favoured Races in the Struggle for Life?*' I would answer, '*The Origin of Species.*' However, not many clients enquire along these lines. Well, none. Most of them want to know (*a*), How long a cheque takes to clear, and (*b*), Have we a public convenience in the near vicinity? Answering both (*a*) and (*b*) for seven and a half hours a day (that's excluding lunch) will, of course, make a girl with less inner resources than myself appear thick and glazed over with boredom. Sometimes I do appear glazed with boredom and slow in response to the said (*a*) and (*b*), but this is because I'm thinking, Was Julius Caesar assassinated in 44 BC or 45? What is the exact spelling of Nicolaus Copernicus – with one i or two e's?

As I have mentioned previously, I am well above average looking and some people have said I'm stunning and my Mum says I could have been a model if it wasn't for my teeth (I have a slight overbite). At school I was particular about my appearance, always appearing well groomed, even during PE. I have worn, for instance, full foundation, toe- and nail-polish, since I was thirteen. At school I paid no attention at all to the formation of oxbow lakes, logarithms, or French adverbs. School didn't really suit my brain. Instead, I studied me.

Somehow I always knew my skin would have to look particularly good under harsh white lights.

At school, in class, under the multiplication and long division tables, I kept myself busy perfecting and polishing my surface: testing colours on my cheekbones, sharpening eye pencils and minimizing my overbite with three quick flicks of my lip brush. I did do homework, though. Well, my own. At home, under Mum's strict tutelage, I learnt calorie counting, crisp ironing techniques and fast stain removal. Nicola, Mum would say, as I read my encyclopedia say, or plucked my eyebrows in the mirror above the sink, how many calories in an apple, a pear *and* a plain digestive biscuit? What cleaning agent would you use, Nicola, to remove spaghetti bolognese from black Italian suede? I have Mum to thank for keeping me in a constant state of alert. What material, she would ask, popping her head round the bathroom door, shrivels *completely* under 145 degrees of heat? At school, the teachers were not aware of my approach to learning, that I had, in fact, any approach to learning. They saw only my apricot lip gloss and heard only the hiss of my hairspray. They missed my intelligence and mental agility (they could have seen that: I have particularly sparkly eyes), and dealt, instead, in heavy sarcasm, theatrical sighs and, sometimes, chalk missiles. All, that is, except Mr Parker.

I always knew that I was special in the same way that some girls know, from the age of five, the exact names of their future husband, and that they'll have twin baby girls called Trish and Martine by the time they're twenty-five. The day Daddy brought home the set of battered encyclopedias I knew that I had found my special gift. Although the books did smell totally horrid (of sour yellow cat's pee), I found I could, on turning to A, not only speed-read to Z, but almost photographically recall what I'd just read. Mum and Daddy marvelled. I think they thought before I was not thick, exactly, but, well, a little bit dim. One day, dear . . . One day I would find that special place where I would shine. It would be, we imagined, a brightly lit place like a stage or a television studio. I would stun the world as though I'd suddenly sprouted wings.

I suppose, in a way, I should thank Mr Parker.

I should feel sorry for Mr Parker but I do not.

Mr Parker was in love with me almost from the word go. Once, that is, I allowed him a glimpse inside my brain. I didn't mean to really. (I'd decided never to dissipate my talent by casual showing off.) It was during History. I was filing my nails as a prelude to painting the tips of them white. This was a style very fashionable in America at the time, well, LA. Mr Parker was rubbing his scalp. In the dusty sunlight you could see it flake. (I could have suggested a useful herb 'n' oil massage.) Everybody else was slumped across the desks or cutting their forearms up with a compass. A meaty bluebottle was buzzing and bashing itself lazily in a zigzag right across the room. It was driving Mr Parker berserk. His loose green eyes were swivelling right round following the buzz. Mr Parker, well, he wasn't exactly handsome. If I say he wore sandals with furry brown socks and smelt of TCP, well, I'm saying a lot. He wasn't popular either. All over school you'd see graffiti like this: TCP. KILL TCP. TCP WOZ ERE WORSE LUCK. TCP was Mr Parker's nickname. It meant, I found out later, 'That *bleep!* Parker'. I always called Mr Parker Mr Parker though, even in his car.

Suddenly, Mr Parker ran down my aisle, clutched my (new) red leather clutch bag and slammed the fly down dead on my desk. 'Gotcha . . . you . . .' he was panting over the blue metallic stain, '. . . *bastard!*' Well, I lost it (well, that stain will never come out). '*Not* bastard, Mr Parker!' I cried. 'That is,' I pointed, 'a male *Calliphora vomitoria* from the fly family *Calliphoridae*!'

I felt Mr Parker's eyes on me all the time after that. I'd be walking down the corridors and feel a kind of heat and wonder then if my stockings were correctly aligned. Applying eye whitener in double maths, I'd see him in my hand mirror peering in, his face pressed right up against the glass. That sort of thing went on for months. I suppose his interest answered a new kind of restlessness in me. I suppose, I don't know why, I began to quite fancy him really.

One day, while I was waiting at the bus stop, worrying

over the spelling of serendipity (I was speed-reading the dictionary at the time), Mr Parker drew up in his little red car and opened the passenger door. The rain was lashing down. I just got in and we drove off, not to his house, he was married, but to a kind of leaf-covered lane. Well, not a lane, more like a tunnel made out of trees, near a river, in a wood. You could smell that river. It smelt. If you dug your stiletto heel in the leaf mould you could see stiletto heels of yellow, very bright, like banana skins. I grew to love that wood. Which was lucky really, as we parked in it for just over five years.

In the spring, the river began to steam and the trees got hazy with budding pale green leaves. The air seemed to wriggle. We'd have a cigarette first, outside, leaning on the red car, and Mr Parker would name the trees, the track of the season on the trees, all the tree diseases and tree parasites, and all the creatures living in the wood, starting up from the one-celled wobbly amoeba. In his car he'd test me. Nicola, he'd say, his hands fumbling on my buttons, or trying to squeeze beneath my white lacy Gossard bra, how would you treat Dutch elm disease? Nicola, he'd kiss me, is tapioca animal, vegetable or mineral? Nicola, what ... ohmygad-*Nicola!* Of course I only let Mr Parker go so far – though, as time passed, I'd take my blouse 'n' bra off straight away as saliva really can stain. Nicola, he'd pant, moving the gear stick, his TCP breath on my neck, pushing against my school skirt, how do you spell bitch? Well, he'd said that once. I slapped him across the nose and slammed out of the car, but then had to get back in again as it was raining. After a cigarette Mr Parker apologized, and we never mentioned it again.

I learnt a lot from Mr Parker, well, a great deal. At home Mum would still try to surprise me in the bath with a question, but she sensed she could no longer challenge me in the old way. I had long exhausted her fields of expertise. Then I caught her looking at me sideways as though wondering when I would fulfil my talent. Or leave home. Daddy spent a great deal of time in the shed now, or slumped in front of the TV. They'd never owned one before: they'd had me to marvel at. He'd look at me sometimes, milky-eyed, as though surprised to see me still sitting up at the sunlamp filing my nails. I was too. I didn't have friends or other hobbies, well, I didn't need them. Apart from the wood, the little red car, I didn't really go out. I left school with History GCSE (I didn't bother sitting anything else), and moved straight into my uniform of starched white blouse with a full white bra flowering underneath. Full make-up but more so, to mark the transition to work.

*

Enquiries (General).
    What two seas are connected by the Suez Canal?
    Mediterranean Sea and Gulf of Suez or Red Sea.
    In which month is the annual State Opening of Parliament?
    November.
    How long does it take to cash a cheque?
    Miss, excuse me, miss, are the lights on? How long does it take to cash a . . .

*

Nicola, Mr Parker said, one day, in his car, in the snowing wood, I'm going to leave my wife. At first I didn't hear him. I was busy watching a robin pull a wiggling worm out of a tree. The worm was skilfully coloured like bark. Which was a pity. The robin craned its neck. Then hopped a branch, tugging. Wet snowflakes fell. Nicola? I felt Mr Parker's tongue. Then his hot damp face appeared from underneath my skirt. Did you hear me? I looked down at Mr Parker then and experienced the same sense of . . . redundancy I now experienced at home. I knew it was over.

Mr Parker left his wife and moved into a bedsit quite near me. Well, round the corner, above the launderette. And each night he phoned and demanded to meet my parents. My parents shuffled about on the kitchen lino, excited, as though they expected great news any day now. Around that time I looked in the mirror and saw two wrinkles, my first, one under each eye, like cracks. I cried so hard that night I thought my head would break. When, I asked myself, *when* would I come into my own? It was the only question I had no answer for. I suppose I went into a bit of a depression.

Ta da! Mr Parker said, ushering me in. In Mr Parker's bedsit the grey walls sagged and sent down a shower of dandruff, well, woodchips. A bleached-out spider plant struggled for light on a desk that seemed a blur of homework and dark scrolled socks and mouldy coffee cups. The single bed loomed out of the corner with the knobbly pink sheets turned back. Standing there with my suitcase, I suddenly missed the wood. Even the yellow pong of autumn, and I found I missed Mr Parker's red car with the condensation running on the windscreen and the icy draughts and Mr Parker trying to part my legs. Mr Parker now expected me to 'do it'. After all, he said, spreading his arms wide, I've given up for you. I need a drink, I said. Which is the first time I've ever said that and the first time I've ever really needed one. OK, one, Mr Parker said, in a new determined voice, and then we're coming straight back here. Yes, Mr Parker, I said. He said, Christ! Call me Alan.

The pub was called The Case Is Altered and smelt of perfume, armpits and chips. It was crowded and so smokily grey it was like we were pushing through resilient sheets of gauze. People pushed me. Mr Parker, scowling, pushed them back. I never really went to pubs. Mr Parker handed me a Bacardi and Coke and took my elbow and shoved me down on a low bar stool. Above me, crackling, I heard the whine of amplifiers, a microphone being first tapped then blown into. And a voice, 'What 'orse—'

Mr Parker said, Drink up Nicola.

'— won the 1989 Cheltenham Gold Cup?'

Desert Orchid, I said, automatically, into my glass. Desert Orchid, someone else shouted out from the crowd.

'Yehudi Moody Menuhin is famous for playing wot musical instrument?'

Violin, I said. Violin, someone else said, a moment later. Up now, Nicola, Mr Parker said. He was pulling up the collar of his coat.

'In our solar system wot type of a body is Neptune?' Um, star, someone said. Planet, I said.

'In astrology, can you name three of the water signs?'

Yes, Pisces, Scorpio, Cancer. I felt faces turn towards me. *Nicola!* Mr Parker hissed.

'What is the opposite of a spring tide?'

A light shone. Neap, I said. Well, I yelled. Suddenly, I was up on my feet: Degas, I answered, Verdi. Lincolnshire. Away from the sun. Slave trade. Potato. Solidarity, Spam. And, as I answered, I felt the floor revolve and suddenly elevate me up, right up into a goldy band of brilliance I've somehow *always known* was burning just ten feet above my head. I heard applause and Mr Parker's voice very tinny and far away. Nico . . . Nicolaaaaa! I smiled like a professional: New Orleans, Hadrian's Wall. Lili Marlene. Fish.

I was in my element, yelling in the heat like I could fly.

# Nerve Endings

The sprout of the nerve is a delicious pain: like a bit lip, or a mouth ulcer the tongue seeks out. It sprouts gradually and then ruffles invisibly.

In middle age she was covered in fine sensate fur.

But, there were pullulating decades to go before then.

Newly single, she found she enjoyed the tap-down search at airports and at quaysides, at the end of red lanes, even when she had nothing to declare. She became skilled at attracting a certain trained uniform attention: she went blinkless like a terrorist. Or she blushed. She did not invite a full naked body search. Rather, it was the sweep of hands under her arms she enjoyed; the T-bar search they made of her skin. She felt an empathy with, and was touched by, the little portable metal-detecting machine: it cried out, like her, at every single scrape of metalloid skin. 'Touch *me*!'

Later, she relied on the circle of rejection and skin-tingling renewal.

When Philip left she found it was the back of her neck that became most affected. The nerve endings there were raw. She had her long wavy red hair styled in a way that required a regular precision cut: a snippy, close-necked shave. Mack, the hairdresser, had such long warm fingers, cool fingernails. He blew the hair-dust from her neck with professional distaste: she saw it spray back in the mirror like shorn red grass. His breath sent her mad. Her spine shrivelled with pleasure and stayed coiled for a month. Blue nerves arrowed up her blood stream, shot through like scissor blades. The nerves on her neck waved. Inevitably, as Mack's cut took on a more deliberate and erotic edge – he made moves behind her like a belly dancer – she became, swiftly, turned off.

She often had a boyfriend (for she was pretty, young, leisured, rich . . .) but, after the first all-over body contact, the first surge of excitement (Touch *me*!) it was as if her nerve endings burrowed back down under her skin and died.

She was called all manner of negative names.

When Andrew left – leaving behind a jungle scrawl, a padded rubber-leafed carpet (he'd filed down all her house plants) – she found it was her right breast that craved attention. Not the nerve centre of the nipple but the right-hand side. Two inches of green-veined flesh. She found herself crushed on public transport, both hands up clutching the hard red plastic strap, a man or old woman, student or tourist, it did not matter whom (though, if they were beautiful it added fizz to her *frisson*) pressed to her side. She swung from the train ceiling, round and round the Circle Line, her breast throbbing swoon.

She went through boyfriends like lunch. They were met with an astonishing gobbling passion. Early on in the relation-ship though, she inspired the reverse: the most passionate and vengeful rejections. She was accused of usury. Negation. All manner of negative names.

Uncoupled, she was affected like a hothouse flower on a rotating plinth. The sun hit her this way and that way, another day, another way; and she'd sprout hungry tendrils of feeling. Buds. Tiny waxy pink mouths screaming: *touch!*

When Colin left (after tipping a fruit cocktail over her head, after snapping her favourite red–gold lipstick), she found it was the tip of her nose that tingled. She made appointments at private clinics, she went for private consultations. Medical men, face decorators, touched and drew her nose. They measured it with a burning slide rule. Her eyes, they noted, in code, were dilated. She sniffed continuously. A severe cocaine addiction would explain a lot. They'd cut the cartilage, operate anyway.

When Paddy left (he fed her goldfish chilli powder), she found it was her toes that demanded to be crushed under strangers' boots, or slipped into shoe after shoe at shoe stores. Her ankle was, later, pleasured in this way too, by ankle chains in a sequence of ankle-chain fitting rooms.

At times, when she had a new boyfriend, and they walked arm in arm through smoky russet city parks, and floppy dogs bounced around them, or they knotted fingers together or made lace that way in pubs, or kissed in tunnel-black alleys, she thought this more ordinary sensation was certainly good enough.

But they would leave.

After many years, after much analysis, it was decided, it was *realized*, it was she who sent them away.

It was the casual traffic of touch that did for her. Money pressed into her palm; a wrist-bone knocking against her own; feeling someone strange steer the base of her spine through a carnival crowd, then disappear.

It could not be bought in an obvious and carnal way, though in times of touch-drought, or when the place affected tingled, as if it would blossom into gigantic garland sores (Touch, touch *me*!) she'd employ a masseur – with a husband's (fleeting) sense of shame. But, it was not exactly the same.

When Mel, in an effort to win her back, sent a gaudy bank of flowers, hairy, tropical shoots, it was the flower boy's pen knocking against her knuckles which threw her back on the couch. When Mel arrived her hunger seemed deranged.

She never knew where the next nerve would come.

It was Frank who affected her eyelashes and sent her fluttering to a doctor, who combed them, his face lunar-huge, and stared at her blank-eyed. Her eyelashes were certainly a little . . . sparse, he said, picking one out, but he had no real explanation for this. She did. It was a favourite trick of hers to glue an eyelash to her cheek. Men, she found, loved to lift or blow it off. She felt their coloured breaths on her skin. Tobacco-coloured, mint . . . She'd enjoyed many such tender displays.

She went to France often to have her cheeks briskly kissed by strangers. This hunger was never assuaged.

In Italy, after John (he'd cut the labels from all her designer-labelled clothes), as she walked in the warm yellow air, she felt her left elbow activate. In Italy she allowed the sons of waiters to tout it to tablecloth after tablecloth. While the elbow throbbed, she grew immensely fat.

In Ireland, after Mark (after he'd unstrung her uncultured pearls, hurled them from the balcony), thin again, her forehead made demands and creased up. It broke out in tears. The manager of the hotel sent for hot wet hankies and stroked her forehead down. He was alarmed by her delirium but, once he'd bent to kiss her, it passed.

As she aged her skin grew more clamorous and thickly coated with nerve fur. She fell over often and had to be helped up. She dropped her keys abruptly, her diamond rings, her credit cards and so was often pleasantly and rudely bumped. She found herself, with a little start of surprise, crushed in a taxi in Mexico City with families and extended families of sheep. A sheep or a peasant breathed heat in her ear. She felt, at the right delicious pressure point, a wool-rimmed, spam-pink, rushing slab of tongue.

When she was too old to attract boyfriends she found, to her relief, that she no longer required the kick-start of rejection. Her skin forgot their names. Her skin fur swayed as tall as corn. The centre of feeling still moved mysteriously over her body and imprinted itself variously, like corn circles. Her ears demanded. Her little toes. The shine on her shin bones.

She began to seek more and more comfort in the medical profession. It was expensive. Her list of private consultations was awesome and crossed the carpet into little red ante-rooms. Her hypochondria advanced. It galloped across continents. One time it was a fork of green vein on her chest. The pulse there alarmed her. Another time it was a tiny freckle in her eyebrow, another in her groin. Another . . . Once she was arrested for lewd behaviour and once she was sent to a drying-out clinic and forced to follow a twelve-step recovery programme. She did not recover. She became an embarrassment to the remnants of her family and friends. A drag on the family's dwindling purse strings. She'd demand intimate touch from strangers, voicing her need out loud: Lay your little finger on my tongue. Touch my skull, honey. Touch me *here*! But the nurses said she was a lovely old lady. She enjoyed, in so far as she never once complained, her bed bath. When they took her pulse or blood pressure, put a finger to her wrist, or stethoscope to her heart, pumped up her upper arm, her face wore a look of such radiant sweetness. When she died she died twice: the first time she simulated death in order to feel a finger and thumb press upon her eyelids. The nurses were startled and then pretty pissed off.

The next time she died was also the first time.

*Remission*

Mick pulls himself up by the window bars of his cell. His biceps bulge weakly. His netted, hair-filled, wide-pored vest strains across his back. The sun shines lemon lollipops of light on his face. Behind him, Warden X leans on the door jamb and exhales great lungfuls of love. 'Visitor for you.'

*

'I think of my little lump,' Lucy tells *Woman's Hour*, hugging her stomach, pausing as the microphone unexpectedly whines, 'as though I'm growing a child. I've decided to nurture it.'

*

'You didn't flipping marry *that*, did you?' Mick sighs in the visiting room, retuning the dial.

Eric sighs too. 'I know, I know . . . But she seemed so, so . . . *doting*.'

She looked nice in his sports car. She had fluffy blonde hair, a snub nose. She was easily pleased. She tanned evenly. It was difficult to list her attractions now. She liked playing house. If only she would *fade* like a pretty woman.

Lucy has been dying publicly for six years.

'I've only got six months,' she sobbed, six years ago.

A life sentence. The weeks passed . . . years.

'I'm in remission.'

'Triffic!' said Eric. And rushed to vomit in the sink. In the mirror he froze on the full electronically lit horror of his face.

'Mmm. Who's the fox?' Distant echo: 'Fox . . . fox . . .'

Eric was *so* . . . handsome once, six years ago: ski-tanned, with a tawny lustrous sheen. Now, his eyes have the salmon pink and dotty print of the *Financial Times*. His chest pants rapidly, comically, like a sick dog's. His tongue, involuntarily, lolls out. He swears it wears a short, Daz-white fur coat. 'Fuck! My tongue's wearing a . . .'

'I think she's immortal,' Eric moans. 'I think someone's given her the gift of eternal life. How am I s'posed to get my hands on her money? I mean, I keep hearing this loud thump, thump pulse.'

'Moan, moan, moan,' Mick says. And spits.

*

'I saw Jesus this morning,' Lucy smiles, in the new giant cottage, in the village of Little Hepping, as seen, thrice, in *Hello!* magazine. 'He was standing at the bottom of the bed and the look he gave me was of, so full of love, I mean,' she giggles, 'I couldn't make an artist's impression of him or anything. What I saw was love. Pure love.'

'Really,' says Eric, and swallows his toast.

He plops a kiss on the air above her pink bald head and sweeps through the house.

Like an arrow. Through the drive, through the village.

Smudging towns. In to the City, into the bank, up in a sec, in the see-through lift. He barks into the mobile phone, the intercom, the Internet, a Dictaphone, his secretary's intricate ear. He makes her earrings jangle freely with nerves. He stops, fused, and looks, forehead pulsing (a great green highway down his head), out through the window, at the opulently tinted pumping sky.

MISERY!

'Lucy's on her way up,' his secretary's Dalek voice grates through the intercom.

Eric, slowly, batters his forehead back and forth against the cold violet glass. Far below, the traffic picks at his beat. He sees himself fall . . . like a Rock of Eric. In ground *rush*. His nose-breath greys the glass: two sniffy wiffs from a tomb.

'Hello darling,' Lucy yells, 'sir-*pri-ise*!' It is not. She arrives each lunchtime positively coloured, demanding treats. 'Darling, lunch. I did one hundred and fifty-*five* press-ups today: feel this.' Eric has to fight the impulse to punch her out.

\*

'I'm not just saying this for effect,' Lucy tells her Health Support Team, 'but since they found it I've felt loads better. Even . . .' her smile broadens, extends to include her pretty, even back teeth, 'sexy.' Her support team smile, edgily, back.

\*

'Wake up, Eric, how do you like . . . *these*.' Twin twiglets in pearly-pink stay-ups.

'Wow,' Eric says, flatly, 'nice.'

In the morning his ears are slopping, wintry-grey, swimming pools of tears.

*

'Me,' Sabine McBrown, his girlfriend, hisses into the phone, 'that's all you ever think about. Me me me.'

Which is true.

Though Eric often thinks: Oh Lord, *why me?*

*Who* could have predicted the media avalanche over his head? Boulders of print. Character stones, syllables dense and descending, scrolling like grey scale, like black snow . . . The swoop-up of Lucy's cancer star. His MISERY began not with Lucy's terminal news (the mushroom cloud found clamped at the belly of her X-ray) but with her hothouse bloom . . . The chewy *stretch* of her remission. Her face now radiates from magazine racks. The phone rings. It's lawyers, it's agents, producers, breakfast TV. They love her pithy plucky style *so* much. Her face is photogenic, her eyes have the moist appeal of veal, her voice sounds mellifluous, manly even, on the radio. Lucy beams. Her skin blooms the silver hue of fruit.

Uncommissioned, just after the terminal shock news, she wrote that *one* article for *GET IT! Good Health Magazine*, simply penned, and now, Lucy waves at the moist green lawns, is modest, just *look*. TV lights bleach the lounge. Soon, she's earning commission on her remission. 'Lucy, you have', her agent affirms, '*fantastic* media viability . . .' An exercise video *Fit to Die*. *A Cancer Cook Book* . . .

'Great news,' the agent screams, 'Elsbeth Carter's got it. Secondaries. Liver. *You*, Lucy McCann, will soon be the nation's sickest sweetheart. ''Rif*fic*!' said Eric, as the avalanche fell on his head.

The postman grumbles up the path, lumbagoed out from the loaded fan bags.

\*

'She *is* immortal . . .' Eric moans, at his teatime tryst, lying in mushed up bed, in the Red Rope Hotel with Sabine McBrown. 'Why can't she just *hurry up* and die?'

Sabine sits up, with a tremor of her supermodel egg-cup breasts. Her eyes narrow.

'You, Eric, are a selfish . . . *runt*. Lucy has got *cancer*, you know.'

'I *know*,' Eric snaps, twanging on his briefs, '*I* know. She *enjoys* it.'

Outside the Red Rope Hotel, Eric stands flaying, flapping in the steak house- and petrol-sodden air, trying to crank up. He sees other fellows flying like arrows home. He sniffs his suit-pits and smells Sabine, stinky banknotes . . . death. Bawling in front of his own eyes, thinking, Why, you pathetic *jerk*, he whirls into a phone booth and rings, using his fingers' digital memory, each single friend. No one's in. He rings North Watford, Mick, old mate. But Mick isn't in. He keeps on forgetting. *The inconvenience!* He must wait for visiting time at Her Majesty's pleasure.

In the visiting room, Mick smokes a fag. The fag is the hardest thing in his near-toothless mouth.

'What I regret most,' he says, 'is the years of dental neglect.'

'Yeah,' says Eric, bored. 'What you in for, anyway?'

'Flip me, you ask! You been coming here for, 'ow . . .? Six, seven, I don't know *years* and *finally* . . . It's all me me me with you. Insider trading if you must . . . Nah, not really. Murder. GBH!'

The idea takes *one* second to form. 'No,' Mick says. 'You've got to be *joking. No* way.'

Eric, as Persuader, has to listen to *a lot* of tales.

*'. . . I had a car, me BM dub, or me Roller. Can't remember which one 'cept it was my white one. Parked it outside my house. All the cars used to get done. I gets a dog, one of them evil smiley cunts. I see the kids prowl. I say, Kids leave me car cos I've got this big, BIG Rottweiler in there. I walk away. I hear this one kid whisper, Your dog, mister, she like fire? . . .*

*. . . I'm on the bus. I see this bloke and he's looking at me. So I say, You looking at me? And this bloke says, As it happens, I am looking at you. So I says, You looking at me . . .'*

'Fascinating,' Eric murmurs as the italics sink on. He chews his lip and looks round the smoke-packed snogging room. Apart from a warden staring him down like a wolf, prison life don't seem so bad.

'If you like it up the arse,' Mick says, 'it's great.'

'Why,' Eric says, with their precise grammar-school enunciation, 'are you talking like that?'

'Because,' Mick whispers, 'I'd be dead meat if I talked like me.'

\*

Murder, Eric thinks, on the eighth anniversary of Lucy's cancer child. The word expands like a helium-filled balloon in his head, squashes his brain round its billowing bowl. Mercy, much nicer. Like doing her *and* the nation a favour, really.

'Darling, I've made your favourite – mmm, scrummy cottage pie!' Lucy interrupts. A tremor of pain ripples both their lips. A sweet sheet of burnt black meat snags beneath the ceiling, beneath the new and amusing load of gold rococo.

''Rrif*fic*,' says Eric.

Through the French windows, on the smoky grey lawns, he sees slugs on the long haul, stoicly trawling their backpacks, leaking viscera . . . Worms fingering up through the soil – giving *him* the finger? Whooping murderously, giving vent, Eric runs around the garden and stamps them out. Panting at the centre of his own blue bloody boot prints, he sees the lawns fissure, go.

'Oh, hold me,' Lucy says, in the night.

No, Eric thinks, hold *me*.

\*

'Dying's been so good for me,' Lucy tells the *Gaby Roslyn Show*. 'I was just a loving wife before . . . before . . . I feel as though I've just popped into a new dimension.'

'Like, frigging . . .' Eric screams weakly at the TV screen, '*Third*.'

Tears freeze on Lucy's fabulous bones. The cameras choke on all there is to lose: the giant cottage in Little Hepping; the clear-honeyed façade, the prettied privet, a Labrador panting lemony breaths, view of a banker ducking underneath a varnished duck sculpture hedge.

*

'She *is* immortal . . . Micksy, oh, please,' Eric says, squeezing out a tear. 'Please. You're out on parole soon. I don't mean hurt. Just . . .' He searches for a couple of nice harmless words, sees a candle go blank, painless, without sound, 'snuff her.'

'Well, let me think,' Mick says, stroking his jaw. 'In the words of Janet Jackson, "And what have you done for me lately?" I think there's a little accounting to do first . . . we were, I believe, eight, and you sat on my chest and fed me worms.'

'Oh, for *Chrissakes*,'

'. . . *My* Slade album. Slag Allen ended up with it. How? . . .

'. . . In 1978 you bought nil packets of fags, and I bought, look at this paper please, that's right, five billion fags. In . . .'

*

'As you die,' Lucy tells Kilroy – and Oprah – 'you receive the gift of love.'

*

'Why', Eric shouts, 'am I the one getting the *shit* when *she's* the one doing the dying?'

'. . . The time you borrowed fifty quid and disappeared for three years. The time you refused to appear for the defence as it would damage your flipping career. The time, after Reading, you told me to ask for a Peter Gabriel haircut.'

'Please,' Eric begs. 'I'm begging ya.'

'Why 'ja *marry* her if you can't *stand* her?'

'I know, I know . . .' Eric weighs up two palm-loads of air. 'All I ever wanted,' he says, lying, '*ever*, is a giant cottage, a blonde. Maybe some kiddies.' Pots of cash. Power. A classy *new* Barbie doll every four years.

'Yeah, well, ditto,' Mick says, also lying, winking an infinitesimal eyelid at Warden X. Warden X expands by the door, he damn near implodes with love.

*

'Lucy's coming up,' says the Dalek. Eric, internally, groans. Lucy enters, floats in beneath a flotilla of gold helium balloons. They fizz all over the room. They fart.

'Aren't they just so *sensational*!' she crows. 'So cheering! I got them from a fan . . . Oh, hello everyone.'

Eric mouths behind a grey bank of backs: '*I* am in a *meeting, Lucy*. A *meeting*!' He stabs, with his tiepin, at a passing helium balloon. '*My*', stab, 'life.'

The big bang sends Lucy out in a head-first, thoughtful skid across the parquet floor. Into the papers. Into a rift. Into a new glossy five-book deal: 'Save Your Life; Now *Save* Your Marriage.'

The lift takes Eric down.

*

'The time you sold my car for me, ha ha . . .

'. . . when you borrowed my Wrangler shirt and I never got it back . . .

'When my mum died and you couldn't be arsed . . .'

'The Liverpool away, when you snogged Nancy Michelson in the Kop *throughout* the match.'

'When you don't phone,' says Sabine. 'When you talk about yourself all the time. When I have to do all the work. When you just lie there floppy like a girl.'

'Mr McCann, we're leaving,' his PA, secretary, and five of his clients say in a block. They leave trailing insults and adjectives: 'Insufferable . . . arrogance, crap, bastard, can't even . . . add . . .'

*

'Please Mick, I'll give you . . .'

'Can't hear you,' Mick hums, humming. 'Gone deaf.'

'FIFTY THOUSAND POUNDS!'

*

Down.

'Leave me', Eric whimpers at various satellite shows 'alone.' Eric sees *her* face on the cover of the *TV Times*.

On the *Pearl and Deane Show*.

Cars drive through Little Hepping at dawn and whisk it away to studios in Birmingham.

Lucy sits up in pancake make-up, her smile brave. She makes the studio audience laugh.

They stand and cheer.

She wins a modelling contract from a famous London wig maker, beams across towns. She looks, Eric thinks, with her pap-white raised ankles and knees, like a twig in a wig . . .

'Leave me alone,' Eric sobs, pressing his palms to the side of his head, hard. Implode, bastard head.

'What's wrong with it?' Sabine asks in the Red Rope Hotel, peering into Eric's lap.

'It's spineless,' Eric moans, 'it's snuffed.'

The postman staggers up the path.

'. . . Men's groups fax regular letters of support. Short stories arrive describing different ways to grieve. Strangers drag Eric further down with pitiful looks. An old lady on the train home bawls, tears pellet off her cheeks. Eric and the old lady sit on the train and scream.

'Fuck,' Eric groans in his sleep, filling his ears up with tears, 'Fuck pulse, bollocks, fuck.'

Down.

The manager of the Red Rope Hotel steps briskly out from his storeroom cupboard to personally humiliate and deliver a short British shrift: 'For shame, your sick and lovely lady wife . . .' Eric arm-wrestles for the room key.

Sabine sobs, 'You're really such a bastard, Eric.'

'But you know I can't *stand* her.'

'She's got *cancer*!'

Cancer cancer fuck fuck.

Sabine whispers, 'Eric, what if the papers find out?' Her face turns ugly with fear.

*

'Mick, sixty thousand . . . sixty-five.'

*

He shoots up to the office in the morning with a skiddy stink of burning rubber. He shoots up the lift shaft. In the board-room, above the mahogany table, he sees, as though through a funhouse mirror, his shirt distorted, his wavering sideburns. A giant green pulse beating down the centre of his skull. Thump, thump pulse.

'Lucy's on her way up.'

Urgh.

Lucy enters wearing a dress shrivelled like a sleeve. 'I just bought it,' she cries, holding the wrinkles out wide. 'Guess how much.'

Eric guesses.

'No, Eric. It was . . .' (distant echo) '. . . *ous*and *ous*and pounds.'

*

'I feel,' Eric says, loosening his collar, 'as though I'm wearing a metal head. Please,' he begs. 'It's not like you're going to heaven, Mick, is it? I'll pay you,' he whispers, shifting a decimal point, 'once the insurance kicks in, one hundred thousand pounds.'

'Think about it,' Mick says, stroking his jaw. 'I must admit, she is pretty sickening.'

Outside the prison, Eric leaps and punches air.

\*

The surgeon says, 'Mrs McCann, I've never seen anything like this. It's, er, completely gone.'

Lucy screams, snatches at her cleared X-ray, 'What do you *mean* ger-*gorn* . . .?'

'I suppose,' the surgeon says, rabbit-faced, 'there may have been some . . . er . . . frightful mix-up.'

'What is', snaps the agent 'this *gorn*?'

\*

Warden X holds Mick's hand. 'I don't want you to go.'

'I imagine,' Mick says, stroking stubble, 'I'll be back here shortly.' He kisses Warden X full in the throat.

\*

Eric lands in red rain. 'Strange.' (Distant echo: '. . . Strange . . . strange'.) His arms stretch and, far below, he sees his hands touch the pavement, rather delicately. A red bomb. A pulmonary embolism. 'What about', Eric says, dying, '*my* fucking remission!'

'Oh,' says Lucy's soundbite, 'this is an immense personal loss.'

\*

The trees make a sound like distant applause. The pale tulips on the funereal path stand like spoons. The soil turns in a rich, moist Christmas-cake mix. Eric sinks straight into the ground. At the impact, everyone, astonished, cries. Lucy sobs because her career in cancer has now been extended by one in grief. Her agent howls as there is really only so-so mileage in Miracles and Mix-ups. Sabine bawls because there is now less chance of being smudgily reproduced by the *News of the World*. Mick tears up because, though Eric was a selfish old git, he was still his good old North Watford mate. Warden X cries because Mick in civvies – he just looks so goddamn *sweet*!

As the sods hit the lid Eric thinks, 'Oh, why Lord. Why *me*?' The early worms begin their tunnel down. Distant echo: 'Me . . . me . . . me me . . .'

# It's the Beast in Me, Baby

Remember that bloke, Shell said.

Celie shuffled through her mental Rolodex of blokes.

The only bloke who was ever decent to me, you know?

Celie frowned while Shell, easily, began to cry.

I thought he'd ring me but when I think about it now, I'm really glad he didn't, you know?

Celie looked at the green cigarillo burning in her hand. At the red lipstick smear. Is that, she wondered, bad-complimentary or bad-clash? Their primary school had been, she recalled, red and green, green and black, block on Lego block. They used to skip, ringlets skipping, down the little school road. Shell?

Two fresh blokes stood by the door. Celie blew a cone of smoke towards them, then another, up and over like a net. The two blokes pointed to the ceiling where the ceiling fans chopped at the smoke. They were laughing, roaring, though the roaring looked false. It was. The taller one, who might have been ginger but had dyed his hair black, like a black satin half-slip, looked straight back. There *was* a gingery tinge around him, but he was cute enough. Celie raised the bow of an eyebrow and twanged it down at her friend. *You* may laugh, she signalled, look what *I'm* stuck with. He was sooo, Shell said . . . cool, you know?

*

Shell first met Simon in a singles bar in Old Compton Street. Later, she sped past him on the M1, catching his double glare, his head down, breaking through a glassy sheet of rain. Was that him on the South Downs, hind legs dragging, just a little bow-legged? He was wearing that *same* red checked jacket, baggy green jeans, brown shoes. Shell was on another date at the time: up and away in a light grey aircraft. As the aircraft looped around Shell saw, through the grimy spin of the window, Simon's face was a blank, oddly vibrating, beige.

In the bar in Old Compton Street, Simon sipped at a pint glass of lemonade. He was listening, head tilting, not to the music box or to the resounding/receding crash of the bar, but to a voice, Mrs Doherty's voice, speaking low in his ear: *Men are like beasts and beasts need to walk. What are they like Simon?* Simon looked through the cloudy sky of his drink. *Beasts*.

*

Shell said, I don't know. There was just something so *different* about him.

*

Shell was attracted by his large still head in the crowd, by his ruffled-up, too-soft-to-spike hairstyle. He wore, on his neck, a pair of the petroleum-blue shades normally worn by orange-tanned skiers. On ski slopes. Strange. As he turned, a chunky brown frown sank at the centre of his forehead like a crucifix. Do you know, Shell said – she waited for a shoal of pretty boys to pass by – I quite like the look of, she pointed, that man.

What attracted me to you first, Shell said to Simon, as they caught the curry-scented 73 bus across town to her flatlet in the village of Stoke Newington, is you don't look reproduced. Those gay boys can look so perfect you know, so *tooooned*. Shell exaggerated the syllables of 'toned', looking at him sideways. Was she amusing? Did he like them *pithy*? Simon smiled. Then, as the bus lights flickered, and black leaf shapes swept in, his smile grew thin.

Shell turned on. In her pink bedroom, she turned on her heavily fringed bedside lamp and began to move in her usual seductive manner, in the pink-aquarium light. She wriggled her leather-girdled end, and, smiling lewdly, flopped down on to her bed. She was actually quite tired. Simon stood for a long moment just outside the circle of light. Light from the hall edged his broad shoulders and large head. His hands unclenched as he walked towards the bed. Hmm, is that, Shell wondered, feeling ice flowing over her guts, fear or desire?

Simon knelt down on the furry bedside rug and pouted his lips. His kiss was cold and wet like the kiss of a child. At first Shell faked total relaxation and let out a little moan.

\*

You know when you lie there like an ironing board? Shell told her friend.

No, Celie said.

Well, I wasn't properly, you know, *relaaaaxed*.

*

Simon kissed Shell. His lips warmed, grew plump. He nipped. Then, as her own lips were just plumping up too, he stopped. His head began to roll in the soft pink air, show alternate profile, this way, then, slowly, that way. He was, Shell saw, pouting beneath him, simply constructed. Oddly symmetrical. His skin was porelessly beige. He had no beard shadow at all. Or, even, nose hair. Strange. Mmmm, Shell said.

Simon shook himself, began to bend towards her . . . Shell closed her eyes. When she opened them again Simon was clicking through the CDs in her CD tower. His lips moved.

Mrs Doherty whispered: *Simon. Men are like beasts and beasts have the energies of man. What do they have, Simon?*

*The energies of man. Find a girl Simon. Do what beasts do.*

What did you say? Shell said. She hugged Simon's chest from behind: Hello you. The words leapt from her mouth and camped at her: *Hello yooou!* She hugged Simon tighter. He was a little soft in the chest area. Bosomy. A little, she said later, *reeaaaaal*. She sniffed and breathed in pine-scented Vosene.

Simon? Shell whispered, I have . . .

He turned round. Shell giggled. She placed a small metal box on the slippy counterpane and twisted her lips down, indicating, she felt, just the right amount of ironic cool. You had to do *such a lot* by gesture nowadays.

Simon looked at her. The crucifix sunk on his head.

Shell broke down: What's the matter . . . er, I mean, we don't have to, well you know, we could just . . . she blushed.

I like, Simon said, Bon Jovi and Elvis Presley, do you?

Er, *okaaay*, Shell said, I mean, yes, I do. Quite.

You ain't, Simon hummed, nothing butta hound dog.

Oh yeah, I *think* I remember that. Wasn't that some kind of advert too?

Simon lay across Shell and kissed her hard. The metal box slid to the floor, making a muffled, faraway plop, like a failed bomb. Simon moved his lips around Shell's lips and slid his tongue quickly in and out. He kissed her mouth hard, kissing for an hour and a half. He kissed her mouth soft.

*

I mean, have you ever been kissed for an hour and a half?

No, Celie said. And yawned.

*

Simon's tongue sunk and swayed in her mouth like a metronome.

Mmm, Shell sighed. Mmmmmmmmmm. She was melting into the slippy stuff of her bed.

Simon turned his head. He said, looking into the distance, through the headboard, affecting suddenly, a transatlantic slang: It's the beast in me ba-baby!

What! Shell yelped.

Well, I'll be going now, Simon said, pulling on his red check jacket.

Oh, said Shell. Her head felt *huge*! Did she feel used? She wasn't sure. I'll show you out, she said, a little huffy, just in case.

At the front door Simon turned back to her and tapped the tip of her shiny nose with a big square finger pad. You're . . . um. You are sweet.

Upstairs, Shell looked at herself in the dressing table mirror. You are . . . *sweet*, she repeated. *You* are sweet. And, yes, she *did* look rather sweet. Her mascara had smudged, making her eyes pool smokily huge. Her lips were bee-stung from all that kissing. Most unusually, her chewing-gum thongs remained unchewed. Because, Shell thought rapidly. I am *far* too sweet to chew! Smiling happily, Shell took her coloured contact lenses out and a partial denture (three back teeth and one front), dipped these two facial appliances into separate sterilized solutions and sank at once into sleep.

Simon snapped on his blue ski-glasses and walked in the pre-dawn monochrome gloom. He walked through crowds of tired killers in Dalston, passed lone prowlers on the Kingsland Road, through stadiums of sleepy pigeons and seagulls in Shoreditch. In Liverpool Street his feet rang off the glittery granite pavements and sent the pigeons up into irritated flight. With his glares on the pigeons turned snow-white. The crucifix on his forehead sunk deep. Simon crossed London Bridge just as the quay lights inked on the water. A perfume clung to him, a musk. He dimly recalled the hard plastic roof of the girls mouth. An oddly smooth contour. He stuck out his tongue. Re-enacted the contour. Strange. He shrugged and walked on.

Simon reached home and said Hello to Mrs Doherty waiting up in the low brightly lit kitchen. Mrs Doherty wore a dressing gown in the same black and white diamond check as the lino. The lino seemed to rise up into her. She placed Simon's cocoa straight into the microwave. Simon blinked. His eyes were scratchy pink slits.

*Did you go to a bar*, Mrs Doherty asked. *Good. Good.*

*Did you kiss a girl, Simon? Good. Good.*

*Remember to say something nice?*

Simon nodded.

*Good man*, Mrs Doherty said. *Men*, she laughed, *you're all the same*.

The microwave pinged.

Mummy, Simon said, toppling, so tiredly.

Upstairs, on the landing, Simon kissed his Mummy's cheek, feeling the kiss sink all the way in.

\*

They're coming *over*, Celie muttered, stubbing out her parakeet-green cigarillo, and reaching for a fresh one.

He was just so, Shell said, on a sob . . . *cooool*.

# *Hearts*

What *rage* when Helen heard an ex-lover was living with another! Although *she* did not love him she did not see why or even *how* he could have learnt to love again.

She looked outside her bedroom window, at the scorched blue and dry green day and, amazing herself, cried. Her tears were the squeeze tears of constipation.

The news arrived in that morning's mail as gossip from an old friend: 'Helen, Ian is shacked up with a nubile gel from Belfast.'

Helen felt unhinged all day and could barely do her gardening. Her brain filled with mental interference, great white TV screens of static. She had intended to fill the long day by planting out broad beans ... and, well – she *still* would! Telling herself off – Get a *grip*! – Helen threw herself into her garden, on to a stack of yellowing newspapers, and began to stab at the earth. Was it her imagination? The earth seemed particularly crusted over today. Impenetrable. She poked with her trowel but succeeded only in annoying a pair of beetle lovers (who had just that moment squeezed off their tight brown hard helmets for an earthy shag and now had to get the damn things back on again). Helen looked up in time to see a fist of black, which was a crow exploding into flight.

She watched that crow pump across the tight blue sky and felt its wing span ripple inside her rib cage.

Ian with another.

Helen went back inside her house and stood leaning her head against the kitchen door jamb. She found she was breathing hard. Very nearly panting. Rosy, her dog, a cringing creature, a white-eyed blonde, stuck her sopping wet muzzle into her hand and rubbed. Simultaneously, the fat marmalade cat, Chops, sidled up and tried to get off with one of Helen's legs. Why did she have such love-hungry pets? They were very nearly nymphomaniacs. Helen, enraged, shook them off (which made them even more love-ravenous) and slammed into the phone.

By midday Helen had acquired as much information as was in the current ether. Ian was living with a former model ('Yes, Helen, you heard right. A *model*!') called Roisine on the west coast of Ireland, and was writing a play ('Yes, Helen, a *play*!'). Postcards, Technicolor shots of the west coast of Ireland immediately slotted themselves in front of Helen's wide eyes. Helen saw Ian and Roisine snogging up against a prickle of black thorn hedge and heard, behind them, the sound track, the crash of a great, green, rollicking spit-filled wave . . . She heard them speaking in Irish, in toy language, saying very clever things about the past . . . They were *breastfeeding each other*. They were laughing, howling by a heap of black steaming peat with teeth shiny-white as stars.

Helen went back into the kitchen, plopped a giant tin of plum tomatoes into the blender and made a bitter bloody mash. She felt the whizz and spume of fury. She ran to the mirror and looked into her tensed face. The whole structure of her skull pushed out. For she had been robbed.

She'd left Ian sucked dry of love. When she'd finished with him, he was a mere husk with embroidered eyes. All he could do was make a high-pitched wailing noise. For six months he'd bombarded her with mad letters, threats, declarations. He'd driven past her house, cruised her at bus stops. In short, he'd behaved exactly as he ought. When the letters, the demented attentions, had ceased, Helen presumed he'd found a corner and died.

All in all it had been a most satisfactory love affair.

And now he was – with another.

The next day Helen drove to her local hairdresser's and had her fine, flaxen, shoulder-length hair dyed as blue–black as her postcard Irish colleen's. Perhaps the crow had also influenced her.

Then she drove to the village boutique Kitz You Out and kitted herself out in a new style: a black woollen dress, pink ballet pumps. The dress was near floor length and had sweet pink rosebuds planted around the neck line. Helen looked in the mirror. This must be what Roisine looked like, only, of course, much better. (If not Roisine, then Roisine's mother.) Helen set a foot out like a set dancer's. Ian, she remembered, had loved, no, *adored* her tiny white hands and feet. (Or was that Keith?) In either case, these were now accentuated by the sea of black.

Helen climbed back into her car, drove on one wheel, sparked rubber, parked outside Stanstead Airport and flew across to Cork.

Suspended across the Irish Sea, Helen looked back at the catalogue cards of her former lovers and found sustenance there. She had reaped very many rewards. She no longer, for example, *had* to work. She had alimony (plural), a body, a bloodied Frankenstein corpse of cash: an arm and leg off one hubby, the head from another. Lovers were plentiful, but it was *she* who was always the one to leave. She left them all broken-hearted. Not once, she repeated this, *not once* had they lived to love again. It was as if she'd sucked all the cell-regenerating love-making sap from them.

Love, she found, was yellow like pure amber but it also had the tinge of earwax. It was inside her and it was so thick. She was thick with love.

Helen, thickened, lowered herself over her aeroplane meal of Irish salmon steak, extracted the white triangular backbone, and dredged the pink sweet flesh through her sharp white teeth. Later, as the plane began its descent, Helen was persuaded that the swill of gin and tonic in her belly was, in fact, the rebirth of love. So, by the time the plane's feet touched Cork she was thoroughly back in love with Ian.

Ian with another.

Ian lay with his other nother in a whitewashed modern bungalow on the west coast of Ireland. The bungalow squatted like an enormous freezer on a sopping wet green rug. In the dark bedroom Ian woke to his new sweetheart and it was *so* sweet. Roisine was asleep on her side and her skin was still sheened by all their rampant lovemaking. They were like furnaces for each other. Their flames were noisy and roared. Ian stroked a strand of Roisine's pale mouse-coloured hair, placed it near his full lips and, moved further along by her pale sleeping beauty, kissed.

Roisine woke and breathed in time with her lover.

Rain; Helen raged. Rain rain rain ... Helen's hired black Volvo cursed its way from Cork, through to Galway and detoured up into Drum Land where the white bungalows huddled in herds from the wind. The hills were dark and shiny-with-constant-wet. Helen shivered over her padded wheel, spiked the road map with her red fingernail. The metallic lakes shivered. Newly formed blue ice in the air cracked as Helen's Volvo crested the motorways and broke through cobwebs of sleet, on to motorway, on to golf course, back to track.

She had to fortify herself along the route.

Kevin Donahue, petrol pump attendant, was amongst the first wave of victims. (He remains struck dumb.) As Helen swung herself back into her car seat Kevin could barely bite down into his ice-cream Mars bar. His breath made frost flowers on her windscreen. Helen looked at him and in the flash of an eyelid she stole his heart away. She tucked it into the glove compartment and drove, plucking, along. Soon that glove compartment was packed with hearts. When Helen reached in for a Polo mint it was as if she'd placed her hand in amongst wet pouting mouths. Drool on her wrist. All the little beating hearts. She plucked the hearts from German tourists, Danish giants, farmers in Kerry ... a bridegroom stands frozen for ever in white wellies; a herdsman stalls behind his shitty-arsed cattle (imagining black Volvos freeze-framing towards him) ... All the little bleating hearts. Helen snatched at vital organs in her spittle-covered gloves. Soon the Volvo was packed soft with hearts and, as Helen wound down the window, she felt the love she'd stolen pump in the tiny blonde hairs on her arms, smoothe the crêpe paper beginning to crumple her skin; Polyfilla the bamboo lines on her neck. Her eyes sparkled and the whites of them made, on every object, the pure splash of bleach.

On arrival in Galway Helen found herself a room in a five-star bed and breakfast and, that night, squeezed all the gelatinous juice from the hearts into her bath. She was beautiful in the oak-framed mirror. Really terrifyingly so. The next day she bought a Galway shawl and a few silver rings with hands on them; an easel, a pot of paints; and with these items crisscrossing her long and elegant frame, she trampled the soft brown ridges of a ploughed field, walked over hill and vale and set herself just above a bungalow so sweet it was like a child's drawing of home.

She painted Ian with another.

By midday she'd spied them. They were walking with a crew of bouncing, happily adjusted mongrel dogs, all of whom were snapping and taking bites out of the air around the couple's head, arms and legs. Ian was holding something that might have been car keys. It flashed. When Helen saw Roisine she saw a twig of a girl with mouse-coloured hair, in piled baggy jumper, grey jeans. Helen breathed raggedly. This was *no rival*. Surely this was a dowdy au pair? For a moment the whole cave of her chest caved it. The sheer *insult* of it nearly flattened her. Ian saw her. She had the joy of watching his hand release the girl's. She imagined, in those moments, he'd sprint towards her, grab her throat, fight with her, then come to that *tensual*, televisual moment between slap or kiss. Kiss of course. Or, she imagined his rush towards her, his sinking knee; she saw his face go red – white – red – waxy – white, while his heart attacked: that new crippled mutant thing he'd grown in place of the one she'd sucked . . .

But Ian smiled pleasantly. He said how marvellous it was to see her. Fantastic. He introduced his shy bride Roisine. Roisine smiled so pleasantly: there was no hint of malice, a whiff of triumph; there was nothing to lock a horn with. Ian wished her a very good morning indeed. He'd hardly recognized her what with the new hairdo, the – he was admiring, but distantly so – regalia. She certainly looked the part. They'd invite her in but they were this moment off to Dublin. Rehearsals, he frowned, you know.

Helen sat on the hill that evening until the clouds on the sky were black on black. The crows flying by were black on black on black. There was a general inkiness, a fluidity to the air which was not just the soft horizontal rain, that made Helen think inky scarves of black were following her home across the Irish Sea, to Stanstead Airport, to the car park, into the familiar scent of her car, where she had to wind the windows up rapidly to protect her throat, where, even so, she began to feel a bit more herself: Get a *grip*!

On arrival home Helen saw the abandoned broad beans had somehow insinuated themselves into the earth and bloomed a moss-green cheeriness right around the cottage. As she watched, their roots began to pull up in front of her face. Show palm. She could almost hear their fingertips sucking and scraping down the drive like a children's game of grand-mother's footsteps. Helen saw her pets, Rosy and Chops, erect in a puddle of light, straining on guard by the rose-rimmed cottage door. Their faithful little faces looked up. With a hoarse cry, Helen ran to them and fell upon their furry necks, their scintillant fur. For a short while, Rosy and Chops eyeballed each other over Helen's heaving, black-coated, broken-hearted back. Then, synchronized, smiling haughtily, prick-eared, tail up, slick-eyed, they *leapt* away.

# *Hard Times*

Was it a pencil or a knife? Could it have been an umbrella-length *sword*?

He saw me coming.

In replay, the fog pumping up from the drains was thick and New-York-yellow. I was walking like a happy fool on the runway of the street, thinking I was one cute sight indeed in my high heels and with the black of the street distilled on my narrow leather back. I'd left my squat house behind, each room like a rummaged jumble sale ... I'd successfully emerged from rubbish sleek as a cat.

*

He took my protective cling film and peeled it off.

'Dear Victim,' the police wrote. Ah, so, that's what I am now.

I am a Victim.

*

I was on my way to meet a gaggle of girls in Dalston, walking, I see now, like a *Crime Watch* reconstruction, in clickety-click heels. I was robbed outside a cash machine, tilted in high heels, dressed for no reason as a trollop, asking the mirror, before I came out, How stupid do I look? Answer from the bleeps of the cash machine: extremely-thick-indeed-girl.

'Don't move,' the Gangster said, 'and you won't get hurt.'

'Don't move and I won't, I'm sorry, ha, ha! *What?* Inside I laughed – though my face had grown curiously slack. Sack that scriptwriter! I quipped (inside). I simply can*not* obey a cliché! But. The Gangster had a knife, the shaft pointing up his sleeve. At least, I *think* he had a knife. The more I replay this scene, though, the more the knife thickens to broadsword, thins to pencil-wide. Could I have been robbed by – a *pencil*? What did I say? Not *HELP!* though *HELP!* howled on my tongue. I said not-a-thing. I punched in my number. I gave him my money. I walked away on jelly-legs, wondering, Funny, how am I walking, moving these arms and legs without a spine?

Rendered passive, speechless. I was *victimized*.

I am a Victim. And, once you're a Victim, the Wankers are *everywhere*.

Let me tell you.

I'm on the 253 bus, on the way to wash seventeen windows (don't ask), on a dirty journey into Bethnal Green, on the top deck, trying to read the TV page, *minding my own business*. There's an agitation across the aisle. A rummage. A small man smiles. I smile back. He is, I notice, rather polished, gleaming like a seal. He is, I notice, clapping. He's clapping now with obscene gesture, he's clamouring for attention. He's polishing, he's – working at a shine. He's . . . It's . . . Oh, my Jesus, it's lacquered *up* like a colonel's stick. 'You *Wanker*!' I yell. For it is true. I look at my watch outraged. 'It's only bloody . . . *nine-thirty* in the morning. I haven't had my breakfast yet.' A dull flush stains my neck. A sick ringing rings. And I'm standing above the Wanker, holding my uncool collapsible umbrella (the one I use only if it really *really* rains), poised ready to rain down blows. My fellow passengers prepare for violence. Time tucks away in a fold. Which makes me wonder. Should I kill him?

*

You ask yourself, *why* is this happening to *me*, why? You reason, well, it's an insane display. If they're insane, mentally not quite all there, it's not personally directed at you. Except, it is. I know it is. You know it is. It is. *The Wankers are everywhere*.

Let me tell you. *This* is not the first time.

I was on my way to sell books in uptown Stoke Newington, loaded down; I was feeling a bit teary (don't ask), I turned to look into an alley. A dumpy man in a granite shadow turned ready to spurt, wearing that Wanker's look of worried pride, his dick in his hands like a thick brown arrow. Which made me wonder, as I shot up the high street, Wanker thoughts: Plug-come, I thought, butter-come or come loose like Pepsi-Cola froth?

Sickened? *I* was sickened. *Who* wants to think thoughts like that? *They* make you think thoughts like that. They make you think like a Wanker.

*

Or:

I was feeling the return of an old dating fever when: I was on my way to a warm*ish* date in Islington, on the windy 73 (please ask). I was in retro-disguise – black leather jacket, red lipstick, hair in a kind of nest – when he, the Wanker, stumbled on board. He was bloated in demented jumper, bum-slid shorts, frog-necked like someone on steroids. He held his dick. It was sluggish and stirred briefly. He didn't work it. Rather, he embraced it with his fist, looked down into its squint eye as if wondering: Is this it? Really?

Yes, Wanker, it is. My anger came out like a genie. 'Why, you . . . et cetera,' I yelled, for still, it was true. I turned to the girl next to me, a sleeping beauty. I said, 'I think it would be judicious if we moved.' Now, I have never said 'judicious' in my life. Who wants to talk like that. *They* make you talk like that. They make you talk like a Wanker.

*

Or they use cunning. They are so very very cunning.

A bad hair day. I was on my way from tea at a friend's new centrally heated flat, head down, stamping through the bus lanes at Finsbury Park, jealous, really gnawed in the guts, when someone blocked my path. It was he. At first I missed the sure signs: pink hand-knitted tank-top, short upper lip.

'Do you want to die?' he said.

I said, 'I'm sorry, what?'

He said, 'Do you want to die?'

He had my attention. He also had black square glasses like all-round eyebrow. 'Oh please,' he begged, 'look.'

I looked. 'Why, you . . . *blah*!' I said. I am cursed with total recall. It was pointy, pink, like an Alsatian dog's.

*

Sometimes, they are supine. They come at you from the ground. *Watch* that ground.

I was on the way to my breakfast café when an old tramp lay, literally, across my path. He was elongated by a black, boot-length, army coat. I was just about to hop smartly across his corpse when a bus pulled in to the parallel bus lane. The tramp muttered, 'Oh save me, help me up,' as though in delirium. What should I do? Someone I knew (friend, enemy) might be on that bus. They might see and report me ignoring the tramp. So, I hauled the tramp up. The tramp hauled back. Suddenly, I'm *on* the tramp. An evil cuddling. His dick pushed in on my fleeing gut. My back legs kicked, thrashed away like a swimmer in a relay race, kicked out pavement spume. I ate dirt. When, finally, I clawed my way free, I kicked the tramp in the guts and knocked his mossy green false teeth out. No. I didn't really. I did that bit in a dream. His dick withered away on his great black coat, drooped like a lonely rhubarb stalk. I got a blunt penknife and hacked it off. No, of course I didn't really. I did that bit in a dream too.

*

Why? You think. *Why* is this happening to *me*, why?

Because I'm a Victim. Well, I tell myself, sod that. No more icey-nicey. No more Mrs Nice Victim.

So, I'm on the 253 bus. I'm poised above the Wanker, with

my collapsible umbrella ready to club in his sealskin head. Time begins again. With each bloody blow I say, 'That, you Wanker, is neither – *bash-bash!* – funny – *whack-whack!*, sexy, nor – *bang-bash!* – clever.'

No, of course I don't really.

I yell, *'Don't move, and you won't get hurt.'*

# There Will Always
# Be a Felicity

Tell me, Hussein said, did she weep before or after?

He didn't want to but he laughed: *During.*

They both rolled. Hussein taking shop-time to roll about on the floor. Gary recovered first.

He saw falling dust on varnish and chrome. On a set of dumb-bells assembled in ever-increasing weights. Shoebox shadows. Stock low on the shelves. He'd been away a long time. On Planet Love. Now he felt emptied. Madness, he thought. It had all drained away from his guts.

He saw her in the building society on his high street, saw her squarely framed like a game show contestant in solid oak veneer. She looked straight at his middle as though she saw his major organs and his veins knotted and coloured beginning to spew sparks like live electrical flex. She was, he thought, rude . . . Though if he saw her on the high street he wouldn't clock her twice.

Bags of money making his pecs and biceps tight, satisfying double thump on the counter, not looking at her, doing his blokey 'Lo doll . . . Starting in when he became aware of her . . . aura, her refrigerated air. A face shaped like a fairy-tale heart. He watched her fingers flick through the notes. The clank of a . . . thumb ring? This detail jarred. Usually, they, girls, babes in banks, girls in building societies (he liked to pronounce, he had theories, polished them up in the shop with Hussein, delivered them later like a comic in the pub: 'Take your average Harvey Nichols girl, she don't drink tea. She's expensive. *Cappuccino.*'), girls in building societies wore silver jewellery, moons and stars, MUM spelled out in gold or MAUREEN. Then, he noticed her lip. Her bottom lip. The indentation. A tiny blemish bruise where a lip-ring usually sank. First, as he sauntered up the high street bulked in his jeans, slightly bow-legged, to the purple columns of Muscle Empire, he felt disgust, then the thought came in: If he kissed her lip-ringed mouth would it be stainless steel cold or would it *warm up*?

He felt as though he'd been shot up through space, through exploding Milky Ways, stars scratching his cheeks like engagement-ring quartz.

He'd gone to the loo and thrown up.

Hussein, banging on the door: Call for you. Then, hissing like a snake through the keyhole: Alert, umbrella alert, it's Felicity.

Felicity called, left messages on his answerphone. He heard her lisp and the spits she sent flying into the phone. Did he want to see *Jurassic Park* with her?

No.

Did he want to meet her at McDonald's for a veggy burger?

No.

Could she just come round?

No. Never. Ever.

He wondered (briefly), as he tugged out till roll, why life

was so unfair. Why he couldn't love *this* girl or even be a little bit nice to her. Why her attentions repelled. Why he'd wasted his charms on her in the first place: bored in the shop one day, flogging her a lime-green leotard on sale for one hundred years. She was pretty with wiggly hair. She reminded him of a sheep. Baa. Could she just baa baa.

Sheep to his dog. *In* the building society twice a day now, completely lost, sometimes three, pretending to beg for change ... Give me ten pounds' worth of twenty-p's pleeze ... waiting for *bleep!* and her green light, letting people queue-jump, panting till he got her, arriving charmless, chatless in front of her cube. His yellow money sacks, due to his general distraction, because he didn't notice Hussein now fisting out fist-loads of cash, deflated slowly, growing saggy like two ageing balloons. Hypnotized, he watched her fingers spark lightning through the cash.

On Planet Love there's so much *time*. Shop days dragged when they used to, he was sure, whizz: babe-watching with Hussein, passing cruel judgements, shop jokes, dressing the dummy Alfredo, catchphrases, shop characters, Wankers and Bastards, Babes and Dolls, ways of signalling hostility with a digital blast of the till.

Drooping, sighing over the counter like a short, swollen sunflower husk.

Chill out, Hussein muttered.

Give me a break.

On Planet Love there is *so much* time. Pavement trees sprouted, flowered, drooped. He ran towards her, pounding the same cracked track under a low umbrella of sky.

He drew blanks.

She never even looked up.

*In* the building society three times a day now, sometimes four. His heart raced. In the building society she would see, he realized, unless she craned her neck, unless he craned his down, only his square blond chin, his bull-neck, his massive shoulders and arms, his chest packed inside his taut T-shirt with the shop logo stamped right across: ENTER THE MUSCLE EMPIRE. Please, he whispered, Obey this T-shirt.

Her name.

Her name tag read Mandy O'Grady. Embossed. Raised. In*sult*! When she should have been called something beautiful, plain, clear, like Jane, Ann. He arrived at her name. It dropped in on him one restless, sheet-wrestling night, like a cold white stone, sending him rippling out: Hope.

Hope.

I hope Hope comes into the shop. I hope Hope buys something and then wants to *try it on*. He imagined, under the louvred shuttered doors, her round silver knees. He endowed her with long silver legs. The rustle of her clothes. He'd forgive her, her beauty would even transcend, he thought, making a tremendous effort, squeezing, blinking with the effort of it, even if she wore, he squeezed, pop socks.

Nothing to do in the evening but lust.

At home he lifted weights in a fever, repeated till his body glistened and his tracksuit bottoms stuck to his legs. He looked at himself in a flattering light. Yellow candles bought in bulk from IKEA, bought especially, once he'd fixed her in a flickering tableau: flat out on his bed. Her long silver body, the lip-ring cooling, gratefully, mournfully, watching him dress. Begging for more? Got to go to work, babe. Totally completely satisfied? Fucking sore.

*

She never even looked up.

He took to wearing shaving lotion, took, in the mornings, to palming it up so she'd recognize his scent, his *hereIam*.

Felicity rang.

Gary, would you like to come to the Freud exhibition at the Whitechapel?

No.

A row on the Serpentine? She had a bottle of pink champagne.

No.

Catch last orders?

Oh, all right then.

In the pub with Felicity he accidentally had a good time. A duet, twin brothers, a saxophonist, a guitarist, played musical jokes: cover versions with thump-thumping base lines; fog-horns through 'Sailing'. A sound through 'Cry Me a River' like torrential rain. The landlord brought out triangular ham sandwiches. Gratis. Gritty sprigs of parsley. Smiled all his dentures. All sealed in together in a ring of fun. Felicity hugged her glass. Her cheeks went pink and swung like two furry apricots. Later, outside her door, he bent down like the pope, majestically kissed her, caught a whiff of her flowered perfume and body spray and hand cream, hair mousse, saw in an instant her stiff new clothes, smelt his own stinky desperation like a blast of heat, managed to snatch his nostrils shut. Baaaaaa. Ran up the high street picturing a new T-shirt: SHOW NO MERCY. Big gap. EVER. Told Hussein: Kissed her, thought she was going to fucking *faint*.

In the window of Muscle Empire he dressed the dummy, Alfredo, in a ruby-red hooded ski suit, made him cock a leg as though just about to venture out on a crispy loaf of snow. Ski's up! Arranged styrofoam pieces to cough on the floor. Alfredo – the Wanker! Hussein joked, popping his head round. Heard the joke clank and fall flat on the floor.

Dear Mandy, he wrote on his paying-in slip, I love you. You are the most beautiful babe/girl/woman in the universe. Kiss me. Yours sincerely, Gary (from Muscle Empire).

Dear Gary, Felicity wrote, just thought you'd like this, cheers, F.

A greasy snack. Mushrooms trapped in egg. He ate it at the counter. Tasted misery and desire and nausea. Threw the note to Hussein. Killed an afteroon taking the piss.

Dear F, Hussein wrote. Gary wouldn't fuck you if you were the last sheep on . . .

Dear F, Gary would shag you if he could gag you if he was desperate, if he could fit into the Model Zadi rubber diving suit, currently modelled by Alfredo the Wanker. Cheers.

Bleep!

Her green light. Love made him senseless, rushing like a fool. He felt his loss of self like a hairy bloody organ flushed by mistake down a loo. He couldn't . . . he did not see why not . . . All other girls loved him. He was cute, chatty, a laugh. The girls in Percy Ingles loved him. The girls in Warehouse adored him. The Asian babes in the supermarket gave him discounts, threw in, sometimes, a free pack of fags, Rolos; he loved Rolos. Felicity left him treats, spider plants on his doorstep. Diana Ross tapes, once a cashmere jumper he had to thank her properly for. They loved him. Wanted a sweet weakness in his legs. Got her X-ray eyes boring holes in his gut. She never even smiled. She read his notes with gun-metal eyes.

Dear Mandy, your beauty makes me cry. (Circled a tear stain, real). Yours sincerely, Gary (from Muscle Empire).

Dear Mandy, I'm 27, unattached, own my own flat (see attached list of things I own). I manage a shop (Muscle Empire) and I love you so much. I've never felt like this before. Yours sincerely. Gary from see above.

He looked in the mirror. If she looked up . . . If only he wasn't *sandy*. He smacked his forehead. Hair fixed back like blond Brillo pads, washed-out like Ken the fucking Barbie doll. He was OK from the mouth down. Blond eyelashes, nearly white, like an albino pig's. Knew he'd gone mad. Really couldn't help driving to another borough, to a chemist he would veto from herein; bought brown eyelash dye. He looked, afterwards, like a cross-dresser crossed. Like a lazy transvestite. Fuck, Hussein said. You look like Alfredo the Wanker.

He did.

It was true.

He posed Alfredo in a Speedo swimsuit. Painted a powder-blue backdrop. Cling film clung to the window, rippled, suggesting heat. Alfredo had his arms up in a triangle, about to dive. But so miserable. Alfredo would never be in a holiday mood. He put a shuttlecock down Alfredo's trunks to cheer him up, no other jokes. Hussein, watching, was jokeless too.

*In* the Building Society five times a day. She wasn't there. She was not ... In the oak cube a gap where Hope should be. A blowsy redhead sat counting out the cash. Potato eyes, a scalding gash of lipstick, ANGIE stamped in gold around her neck. In*sult*!

No Hope the next day or the day after that. Or the day ... Howled in the shop, hurt in his flat, at the counter of the pub, like a dog, like a yellow-eyed prairie dog, lonesome as fuck.

Felicity rang.

Did he want to go to a Phil Collins concert? She had a spare ticket.

No.

Did he want to eat Pizza? Her treat.

No.

Did he want ...

Look Felicity, tried to temper it, breathed deeply, too late, *shut the fuck up*.

Lispy sobbing on the line. He felt like shit.

Mandy, Miss O'Grady, was on holiday, he was informed. No, she wasn't hiding round the back. *Sir, you can't go in there sir*.

Back next week. Greece.

Imagined her there with Alfredo the Wanker. Sizzling like bacon on the beach. Wished he hadn't endowed Alfredo quite so much. Shook himself. Get a grip. Alfredo is a dummy. Like you.

Trumpets. A blasting sound like tired Vikings on the last stretch home. Though he knew this moment must come. Islanded on pavement. He saw her out on the high street, alone in the evening, in a cone of bus-stop light: sexy black grunge, face cast in bronze, hair spouting like a shot of frozen water. Lovely (thankfully), from the waist down. Ma . . . Ma . . . Mandy! He walked towards her, bulky arms out. She would just fall straight in . . . Saw her mouth open, the lip-ring in place. Didn't hear the word she spat. Formed it later out of shards of air: Creep. Get lost Creep.

Felicity, would you like to come round?

Blocked. Up to his neck in come. Get round now.

Fucked her till he fell apart halfway through. A restless, sheep-wrestling night. Unlikely couple paw-pawing the pillows: howling, baa-baaing; legs sunk in a lake of sheepdog tears.

# *Heavy Petting*

*(For Tiny and Twinkle)*

I come from a long line of pet deaths. Bunny and Clyde . . .
Tiny and Twinkle. Sid and Nancy. Mungo . . .

But it's Godfrey who haunts me.

At night, when the cistern gurgles, it's like he's back with
a splash.

Majella hooped him at a fairground and brought him home,
dangling from her thumb, gulping mist in a plastic bag. He
wasn't expected to live for long. She plopped him in the dead
terrapin's tank: watched him loop. Blessed his tank: named
him after her ex-fiancé, the paratrooper, the one who'd
chucked her out on the street, howling. Godfrey.

Godfrey was like Godfrey: he was quick, ginger, flash, but
he was never mean.

He was so *bright* in our dingy house. He blew air kisses all
day, puffed out silvery smoke rings . . . link chains. A stray
sunbeam hit his glossy water and he sparkled. Round and
round: an endless U-ey . . . At first, Majella blew him kisses
back, showered him with presents from the pet shop: bright
coral-gravels, a pagoda, a stone-coloured hide'n'seek boot, a
fluorescent pink plastic hanging garden . . . and sieved him
out, with the tea-strainer, for long transatlantic journeys in
the bath – and then she *turned*. She turned to clubbing,

drugging, and a bloke called either Mr Ecstasy or Marv. Or both. Majella, my sister, went *rave* mad.

One day Majella was a laughter-line in a nightie, spitting on an iron, singeing a pleat down her navy work skirt; and next, she was this gum-snapping *stranger* pacing up our hall: wearing tight T-shirts with daisies on them, calling cabs at midnight; hipped out, with her belly button sticking out of flab. (Later, she had it pierced: it went septic. Septicaemia . . . She got gangrene. She had to go to hospital. It went the size of a yeasty currant bun. But that was *much* later.)

Majella really *loved* Godfrey but, after she hit the clubbing scene, got, as she called it, 'loved up', she hated him.

Listening outside her door I heard her chant above her telly, 'Ignore me now army boy. You *bastard*. You *bastard* Godfrey. What are you? *You bastard* Godfrey . . .'

I didn't think pretty Godfrey could live for long.

*

I was studying for A levels at the time, training hard as a Young Novelist, honing my powers of observation in little red note pads. (When I got my grades, the predicted A, A, A, I'd get to university five hundred miles away: leave home without one look back. I had to stay focused, unattached.) But I couldn't resist saving Godfrey. One wriggle in his tank, and I was hooked!

'Mum?' I said. '*Look!*' I'd airlifted him out from the hell-hole of Majella's bedroom: blown away his sky of talcum powder, reeled out a foot of Majella's tan-coloured, scummy tights, and set him down by the scummy cooker in the kitchen. Though he was thin – a red bone in a white sock – he was, I thought, *all the light in our house boiled down*.

In the hot kitchen Godfrey blinked his gold. 'Look Mum,' I said, 'isn't he *sweeeet*?'

Mum looked down: her cheeks steamed, flushed like two rubbed spots. Her eyes, under her sweaty eyebrows, gleamed. I looked from her to the brown sudsy cooking pots, back to Godfrey, back to Mum.

I thought: Poor Godfrey, he won't last for long. Out of the fire, into the pan.

*

Mum had gone . . . funny in the head. That's what Majella yelled, tapping her temple: 'You're *funny-in-the-head*,' as though Mum's head had been stacked (when we weren't looking) with comic books, sitcoms . . . I couldn't think of a better explanation myself. As I noted, in my novel-training note pads, when Mum *went funny* she went like Majella: *like that!* One day the air was a soft brown wall of unflushed loos, rusting geraniums, takeaway foods. Dust snuffed from the carpets thick as bonemeal. All day Mum made secret-recipe soups: threw great slop waves across the lawns. She'd scour the cupboards for odd ingredients. In went Majella's old school tie, an aubergine, one cake of cherry shoe polish . . . Out puffed rust and rubble, smells that made the plants cave in.

Outside, our other pets howled on the lawns, sang like exiles, made a heady high white noise, scribbled their nibbled light pink legs in the sheds, kicked up for dinner time. The toy poodles shook their pale dreadlocks. Our albino rabbits stretched their dirty jaws. Across the neighbourhood, strays joined in: cats caterwauled. Mum stirred away in the kitchen. She boomed a silent radar: her animal attraction. The pets on the lawns crackled, eared up and somersaulted back. Or they'd bounce and pose above the grassy gore, suspended for a moment, hunched like fridge magnets.

In his tank Godfrey (plumped up), beaming bright, would pause. He'd leap above the pagoda, hang out in the hanging garden. Dirty strobe light smacked his back. His tail thumped. He swam on.

We had to ring for takeaways. At night, when the cat songs got too much, I'd lob our leftover cartons of chicken tikka, the chewy rinds from our takeaway pizzas, salty chip rejects, up out and into the long splattered grass. Shrieks! A scrummage. A feral pet race. The air filled with clods of earth: back-kicked peas. Tree-high stalks shook. As I noted in my red note pads, only the *very* fast survived.

*

Doctor Trang upped Mum's medication. The side effects, he said (zombie-ism, intense communion with small dumb animals), was a small price to pay, believe him. I did. I'd already noted the symptom: synchronicity. In the hot kitchen, when Mum paused, holding a ladle, Godfrey paused too; when one stirred, the other whizzed rapidly round.

In the kitchen Godfrey's light drew me to him. He surfed the surface; flayed gold . . . green . . . red. His tank bubbled like a miniature jacuzzi: full of air and spinning fat globes. He'd flip on his side, fin a zippy sidestroke, blow a little link

136

kiss at Mum as she sipped, with deep concentration, at her wooden spoon. Mum looked down at Godfrey and blew him crumbs, a grape, a rubber fish face. They were one.

At least I knew, with Mum around, Godfrey was safe.

At night, dust snowed around me. My plimsolls squeaked on the sticky lino. Never mind, I told myself, opening my revision notes, I'll be up in Loughborough soon . . . maybe Edinburgh. Wales. The University of Ulster? Miles and miles away . . . Somewhere clean. I vowed then, catching glitter scales from Godfrey, a tinkle tune from deep down in the blue pagoda, when, eventually I escaped, Godfrey was coming with me too. 'Godfrey,' I urged, '*stay* strong.'

'Manchester,' I whispered. 'Newcastle. Durham . . . You, Godfrey, and me.'

At night, our other pets sat in line on the black grass: ruby-red-eyed. They were the lifers: all born to us, given to us, at a time when we must have seemed, no, we were *exactly* like a photograph happily framed: there was Mum in rose-tinted C&A blouse; Dad, roastily tanned in his crisp blue cotton overalls. Majella and me in a our steam-ironed bottle-green school uniforms (Majella's big hands on my little shoulders), showing our heavy-metal orthodontistry. Behind us surged a thunderous studio sky. Around us hopped the albino rabbits, the tortoise. The mongrels. The cats. Poodles . . . They all began to die.

Majella started clubbing it once a week, then twice . . . thrice . . . Mr Marv was a light voice on the line (a 'Yeah', a 'She in?'). He was a slice of shadow, a stripe of Adidas in the crack of a cab. Majella came home shiny, she sniffed, snapped her chewing gum at Godfrey. (Her luminous inks flowered first in the choke of the hall.) In the kitchen she drank tap water, spat green tubes of it through gaps in her teeth at me, at my homework; stared in at Godfrey as he flashed to and fro in his tank. Her face greyed, grew stone. She hovered over his tank, dribbled strands of her long beige hair in, eyes set wide apart: black-pooled, scary, like a shark's. Godfrey cowered in his hide'n'seek boot. I cowered too. 'Godfrey,' Majella chanted, 'I'm going to *get* you. What am I going to do Godfrey? *Get* you.'

I didn't think Godfrey could survive for long.

Mum filled up pots, slopped the rejects out in long brown rattling arcs. Soup skin wobbled on the grass, shone like satin wheels. Pets raced from the sheds, squacked.

In the kitchen her pots heaved. A carrot went in. A bicycle pump, a jagged tin ... Mum had the radio tuned to LBC. Godfrey swam rapids in his tank. His jowls flopped. His movements grew fevered. His tail rudder really whipped froth along. His little face, pressing flat for a moment against the glass, began to look quite – sad. Perhaps it was Majella? Ceaseless LBC? A tiny slit in Mum's synchronicity? Flitting across his features I'd see the face-mask of an ex-pet: one of the terrapins: Sandy? Andy? . . . One of those who'd dried. Outside on the lawns, all the pets cried.

*

In my trainee note pads, I noted, sipping a Lemsip, 'We're all on medication now.' Mum had little white pills. Majella had her little white pills. Even Dad, who I was in love with, took massive painkillers. He had migraine. He'd come home from the railways like a train. Light stabbed him. Coffee killed him. Pineapple juice made him cry. He had migraine so bad he had to inject himself in the bathroom, using his leather belt as a tourniquet. (His injection kit was a toy briefcase, deadly black; inside, chrome cylinders, needles so thick they made your skin lock.) He had blinders. He'd charge home honking noise, smoking rust, with one eye spinning like a shot blue marble, the other scrunching up his forehead, his bobble hat thick with dust. I don't think he noticed the litter under his boots, or chicken tikka again for tea. I stood in the kitchen sipping blackcurrant Lemsip, studying my books, peeping in at Godfrey as he swam round . . . round.

Godfrey swam. He swam in brackish oily water and then, it seemed, he was deep in soup. He paddled past florets of cauliflower, dived under broccoli bombs, breasted logs of carrots, stinking shreds of chicken and lamb. He moved not in water but in stuff he really had to fin through. Gaspacho. The air flowed with stock. Godfrey gave little shivery, fastidious leaps. Mum, stirring, leaped too. Leaning, trying to talk sense into Mum, one day, yelling above the radio blah-blah of LBC, I saw Godfrey take a leap at the edge. But the walls of the terrapin tank were too high. He leapt but a stray *calamaro* ringed his neck, winched it back, cut his arrow-like route to the floor. My heart flipped. Godfrey's battered, swollen, mottled, white-veined mouth glugged each time, sank to blank – down amongst the greasy olives, baggy purple prunes, hairy anchovies swishing by like unshaved legs: the assorted

mucous beneath the murk. I'd mumble above his surface:
'Leeds . . . Aberystwyth . . . Godfrey, you hang on.' I changed
Godfrey's water but Mum souped it straight back up. I tried
putting Godfrey in my bedroom near my computer and neat
stacks of homework but Mum kept bringing him down,
sloshing, bashing his delicate lips brown. I tried to keep
Godfrey on the up.

But I failed. I failed my mocks. An (un-predicted) D, D, E.
When I told Godfrey he flickered away. I looked for him in
the grey TV screen of his tank. 'I'm sorry, Godfrey,' I said. I
turned to Mum. She stirred away.

I tried to stay focused, stay head-down, but . . .

I thought Majella was now heavily into the drug scene, was
like a suburban drug queen, and I was worried. In the high
streets, on Saturdays, she walked like a celebrity, in dark
glasses, like *Ms* Ecstasy, grinding from the hip. Cruddy people
tried to talk to her. Hordes of dirty, whey-faced kids whispered around her, begging for crumbs, for 'disco biscuits'.
Majella brushed them off and, with a swing of her shiny nylon
ginger hairpiece, a flick of her reddening belly button, she
mooched away. She had loads of money. Notes fell around
her, folded up, tiny.

I saw adverts in the papers for people to appear and confess
personal family information on *Esther* or on *Vanessa*, and I
was thinking of appearing. I'd snitch Majella up for her own
good. I'd get her into rehab. Write to her from my tidy room.
I circled the adverts with red biro and left them on Majella's
littered grey bed, as a warning, a hint for her to *pull herself
together*. I tapped Mum's arm in the kitchen. 'Mum?' Godfrey

paused. 'Godfrey?' I said. 'Newcastle Polytechnic? Brighton FE?' Godfrey swam away.

\*

Majella started clubbing it four times a week, five. She'd come home at around four o'clock in the morning, with Mr Marv. (She'd sleep maybe two hours, then speed off to work. Her eyes were like slots.) I'd wait up, reassuring Godfrey there'd be no game-playing tonight whatsoever, watching as his sides bulged at the scrape of a key ... Mr Marv swung in first: smirked, picked up a dirty fork, toyed with its crusty prong, slid it up his sleeve. Majella doubled behind him: they were thin, shiny, daisy-topped. They'd sloppy-kiss, edge to the tank; rub each other up, but I was on guard, stayed solid, watched for the sudden lunge, the stabbing fork. They'd kiss out. Then, without warning, double back, *crash* into the kitchen tooled up to play, in between licks and despite my protestations, the Get Godfrey Game. They forked but Godfrey dived under the blue pagoda. They stabbed but Godfrey ducked into the hide'n'seek boot. He whizzed rapidly around a roast spud. Watching his dive I *felt* the full surge of his life force: he'd leapt back from a death wish; got firmly back *into* the swim; he swam away. Majella and Marv forked up sodden Coco-Pops, fried clumps of wire wool, crumbless stiff blue fingers of fish. Godfrey lived to flicker away.

\*

Godfrey survived all through Majella's Marv stage, her Darren & speed stage, her LSD plus E stage. His stroke became really butch, determined. His nose grew blunt from speeding U-ies against the glass. Majella went clubbing six times a week. She looked thin-skinned. I could see the blood network through her face. She'd come home haggard in her Nat West uniform looking forty years old and emerge from her room, hours later, remarkably refreshed; showing tight arse-cleavage, her cheeks sparkly like two just-peeled spuds, her hair with a wide road of centre-parting, looking *just* eleven years old. In a rare burst of sisterhood, once, she showed me the three moves I'd need should I ever give up being a 'snitchy-bitch' and take up clubbing instead:

1. You put your fingers in the air and stab as though you're telling someone to piss off a lot.
2. You dance like snakes would.
3. You maintain an ironic hipster pose at all times.

But the music didn't really make sense to me: it seemed to consist of just the *one* sustained note and then random others! I couldn't see the point in all the drug taking. I preferred, as a student Novelist, the occasional Lemsip, a paracetamol for my increasingly tense and nervous headaches, and life in the raw.

\*

Our other pets went funny, *funnier*, in the head: showed acute symptoms of distress, neurosi, when they heard the squeal of a taxi. They bounced up and down on the grass, paced two steps forward, two steps back.

At night, sitting up with my computer, I'd hear Majella

come home with a club drone, a Clive, a Tyrone, a Jeff . . .
and I'd wait for the screaming to start. A yapping; barking.
Squeaking. Flash of a penknife. Then, the rabbits would start.
Carnage. Lights snapping on and off in the neighbourhood;
the grass electrified . . . shapes darting in and out of the sheds.
One night I saw Mr Marv, Clive and Majella wipe blood from
their mouths, a bit of white fur, a ridged bone, streaking
through the grass, and I fell back on my bed and thought: I've
got to leave this family *now*. I had to keep racing down to
protect Godfrey from the Get Godfrey Games. In the kitchen
Majella stabbed at his tank, screamed out her old howling
rage, stabbed, as though Godfrey really was her *ex*-Godfrey,
the keen-eyed paratrooper; as though she really expected a
thick hairy wrist, a fist of fat freckled fingers, to spring from
the tank: *Attack!* Godfrey ducked and dived, slithered and
writhed: survived. On bad nights Mum had to run down in
her nightie to quieten the dawn chorus squacking up the pear
trees, squalling from the sheds. She'd raise her long arms and
shush the insects lying crippled and crying on the broken but
still-swinging greasy black grass. The cats and dogs, the rabbits
and shieldless peeled tortoi staggered up the bloody garden
paths to have their wounds licked.

Summer was awful. I failed my A Levels and then I failed
my resits (Fs). Tiny died in the sheds (she was all loose inside,
really awful, like a bag of curds), and then Twinkle got run
over. The tortoi fell into a coma and died. Suzi developed
some kind of tumour on her neck and started going for Dad
as he stepped in through the door from work. Really for *his*
neck. Like *flying* through the air, like hiding under the stairs

or crouched in the airing cupboard like Patience on a stack of dank sheets ... The vet said a tumour removal operation would cost about forty pounds. One day I came in from signing on and Suzi wasn't there. Dad said she'd gone: 'Doggone.' He'd probably let her loose on the motorway, the bastard.

So we only had Godfrey left.

And Godfrey was getting bigger.

He lived on juicy blue flies that fell from the ceiling and cod in butter sauce. He really liked chips. If you plopped a chip in the tank Godfrey gobbled it down in one, like a piranha. Godfrey was so fat now he could barely turn around in his tank. He swam on though. He only paused in his heavy front crawl to listen to Mum's long radio monologues or watch her manic hands chop the air. He still blew her kiss and kiss kiss. Mum gleamed. She poured old cups of sugary sun-warmed tea on his back to keep his water level up; pulled a few rubbery fish faces; flipped in chips. With each look-in Godfrey swam with extra verve; blew out kiss and ... kiss and ... kiss. Sometimes, Mum kissed back. As the kitchen boiled up, Godfrey's tank became just like another steaming bowl of soup: he smelt, sometimes, really tasty.

I wasn't so happy then. I tried to keep my spirits up by writing an epic novel slowly by computer in the morning and swimming slowly in the swimming pool down the road in the afternoon. I was quite good at breast stroke and, as I breasted the clear blue water, I thought about Godfrey: his immense powers of endurance, his selflessness. I admired the sheer *purity* of his direction. His staying power. I would, I told myself, now eschew all Lemsips and paracetamol. I would be as Godfrey, and simply *endure*.

Dad started coming home late, becalmed, with rust marks like vicious love bites on his neck. I noted his clothes no longer billowed their usual bluey-grey cloud of concrete dust. Had he shaken it elsewhere? I thought: Yes. (I imagined a bottle-blonde in a nylon cream cardigan donned like a cloak . . . I drew a picture of her in my notebook, stabbed big juicy blackheads into her chin.) His boots also had new bootlaces on them. I swam and listed clues like that. I was even more worried about Majella. I could *smell* her rotting flesh. It smelt light green. I'd be up guarding Godfrey, watching late-night Hindu films on the telly, waiting for dawn to crack light across the old chicken tikka cartons on the still black lawns: I'd wait for Majella to come home. Majella staggered from her cab. I'd smell her first: rot. She'd come up daisies in the hall, push straight through me, sneer, throw the drug literature I'd got from Dr Trang back in my face, push me off. Her forehead and temples were glossed with sweat; above her hipsters the belly button rose from its punctured hood like a lump of red, still-cooking, bread. 'Majella?' I called. I had Dettol on hand, TCP ready. Majella staggered past me, zigzagged up the stairs, shook the light fittings, and slammed a heavy screen of dust from her door frame.

Godfrey swam in his tank. Gulped, slowly, round.

Mum's medications went haywire. She was talking more or less out loud: answering all the voices chanting inside her head. Under Dr Trang's direction she had to swallow his pills and lift her flabby grey tongue for his inspection. Mum swallowed. The muscles in her throat rippled. Dr Trang shook his head, perplexed, and wrinkled his nose.

Mum talked back to LBC on the radio, nodded vigorously at whichever other airwave was tuning her in . . . fuzzing her out. A new pet fan squeaked from the bread bin: a pet mouse. The mouse begged at her heels as she stirred the soup. Or it climbed on to the beige stubble plains of her worn-out carpet slippers, shiny pink mouse marigolds signing up supplications; squeak plaintive. Mum stirred the soup. The mouse scampered up her leg, her sleeve, her muscled arm, on to her shoulder, turned somersaults, squivelled hips, squeaked for attention, its cute black persistent eyes gleaming. Mum stirred on. The mouse cut a squeak through her airways. Godfrey, in his tank, splished up distraction: wacked up prawns, corn on the cob . . . splashed. The mouse tricked on. Wandering into the kitchen one hot afternoon, chewing my hand, I heard a – different squeak. Human: 'A carrot IS essential, mango chut—' The mouse was poised up on Mum's thumb, paws in beg mode, raised so its whiskers could tickle her own. Mum was squeaking, in a squeaky Nice-Aunty voice, the secret of her secret-recipe soups. She roared: 'Vanilla essence obviously, stupid mouse, ha ha ha fluff! One cornflake, leather thong . . .'

Godfrey broke surface. Red-eyed. Slowly dived. He no longer got a look-in.

Mum petted the mouse. She bound it to her gold wedding band, confided sauce notes at its peaked and quivery carpet-felt ears; *wheeed* it through a PEAK–trough–PEAK roller-coaster ride of brown kitchen soup air: all day. Or, with no warning, she leapt decibels: SHRIEKED! Godfrey swam on ignored, like me, up and down. Up and slowly, solidly down.

\*

By day, stinking of chlorine, I wrote out job applications and listed my Reasons for Application. Sometimes I sat in my old dark-green school uniform adding a new chapter to my opus: Chapter 67 ... Chapter 110. Or I'd look through my thumbed, smudged A Level text books and wonder how and exactly *at which point* I failed. At night I stared into Godfrey's tank and synchronized with his one thought: Swim *on*. Just *swim* on. *Swim* swim swim.

Then one day I came home from a dole recall interview, chewing my lip. I thought I'd just look in on old Godfrey and start a really pure and positive Zen afternoon: Go on. Just *get on*. Chapter 200. Chapter 201 ... I caught Mum leaning over Godfrey's tank. She was sly-faced, hugely pored. Her mouse-fan was boxing with excitement, shrieking squeaks from the bowl of her collar bone; it leapt at her stiff ponytailed head, climbed her ponytail scaffold. Wheeeeed round. The mouse grinned as Mum, gum frilled, tippled and dribbled the contents out of her brown pill bag.

The little white pills slid on a slide through Godfrey's murk, became, I noted, with their powdery star tails, like ultra-white planets in flux. I saw Godfrey, buoyed up by half a cheese'n'viscous roll, by a boiled egg, pickled and embryonic like new baby skin – pause. The planets glazed his right side-eye, shock-waved, rearranged. You ... *good* Godfrey, I urged, Ignore. Just swim *on* ... Godfrey. You *swim* on! Godfrey swam on, swam and swam on till, with a flash of tail rudder, a shiver, a final soup-thwacking U-ey, he – gulped. His throat rippled and he gulped again.

I went into the garden and, lying out among the stale pizza crusts, with big raindrops splashing on my forehead, I began to cry.

Godfrey lay at the bottom of the tank, slowly burbling, like a miniature ginger whale.

*

Doctor Trang gave me pills. I had growing pains, he said. He patted my hand kindly and suggested I wash more. I smelt a bit fishy. I was a pretty little thing underneath all those eyebrows. I wandered the high streets, up and down, as the drugs made me march, and thought about a new novel I would write by hand, using pencil. No more computers. I'd get back into the raw.

In the kitchen, Mum shouted at the mouse-fan and the mouse-fan ran to fetch a friend. The two mice looked up and nervously conferred as Mum ranted and confused them, sent a pea-green football flying off her wooden spoon. They chased.

I bent my knees to the tank and looked, with my slow-motion blink rate, into the thunderous grey matter where something large and orange glowed. 'I forgive you, Godfrey,' I said, reaching for a fork. 'I'm . . .' I stabbed, stammering, 'o-out of it ta-*too*.' I smelt light green: saw, on my periphery, luminous daisies bloom. 'Godfrey,' I said, 'the ga-game is o-o-ver.' Godfrey bellied up. Beside me, I heard Majella sob.

# *A Little Living*

In the park the trees spin like ice dancers, whoosh! That wind is whippy as fuck! It's a seeking wind. It's seeking me. I feel, through the loose window panes, its icy lick on my skin. Will it be me, Barry? Yes! It's got me, Barry, on its suction pads ... Fingers ... cling to the table. Cheeks strain ... bounce down around the flats. Be-yong! Dong! Bounce on concrete, off rubber-plated sky ... In the kitchen, I look at Drew's face. I loom close as a ghost: my ectoplasm sinks right through her morning comic horror yarn. She's zigzagging across a page, absorbed, chewing a string of her dirty blonde hair. Does she know there are no blondes left in America? None. It's here in bold; in boxed-in fact. I'd tell her, I'd certainly let her know, but we are agreed: no talk at Start of Day. No talk at End of Day. Just two of our little living rules ... Toast crumbs dot her mouth. The T-bar of her face is practically aglow. Heck, I'm reflected! Is that any way to keep your man? I look at my pamphlet once more. At the next fact down. The amassed inky evidence seems, no, *is* incontrovertible: there are only SEVEN places left in heaven. And me, Barry, I am having one of them. How to get on that fast track to heaven? *Whoosh!*

Drew leaves for school, late (she's a schoolteacher), as I file my pamphlet under A for *Agh!* I take a bath, thoroughly soaping my whole body. I look at my bubbled skin and address it thus: You, body dear, are a frothy little thing and yet you are my vehicle through life. Hmm. My body lies clearly unrevved, stalled by my homage. Bubbles pop flat. Is it a shy thing? I have not noticed any symptoms of shyness. It is certainly a pale green horrid-looking thing. The legs fork up like tooth roots. How to get my root a root in heaven? Believe me, I'm occupied.

Drew rings mid-morning for a wifely chat. A little itinerary chat. I snap and crack the phone down. I've got a busy day, Lady. It's mapped. In the park, under the ice-skaters, I narrow my eyes to slits. There is something . . . different, something not quite . . . There are no flowers in the flower beds! I spin with the trees. And the ducks! The ducks no longer have interesting foliage to duck into! Why not? Of course I know the answer already and so now I'll be a right clever bastard indeed: because the council is *far too poor* to put park in the park. But is there, and I think there is, somewhere, a council flat garlanded with flowers? Our mayor a-splishy-splashing in a weed-strewn bath? Perhaps. I pause, panting. I look at the twirly strands of anaemic grass and see, through my X-ray contact lenses, the busy lives scurrying about the planet. And, in that pause, I feel the whole wide *race of the world*!

In the park café, exhausted by my vision, I order a CUP OF TEA PLEASE from the brain-damaged girl behind the counter. We go through the following rigmarole while a vein, thick and green as varicose, as pea soup, pumps, mesmerically, on her nose. Pump. Pump. Frowning for thought, the girl sets before my tea-ringed throne a foaming glass of milk, one completely fizzed-out glass of cola, a cup of coffee, one cappuccino. This is an interesting disease: CUP OF TEA does not compute. I fill my bladder with her free gifts, quite enjoying my scan of her flaky blunt eyelashes, her slither of cucumber lip. Why, I'm thinking of asking her out for a date.

This is what my life is like in the late twentieth century. It's caffeine-rich.

The afternoons are a problem. (See P for Prob.) I grab the 253, or it grabs me, and I'm hurtled like a pea down a pod to my afternoon destination. This bus kicks dust. I catch a matinée at the Odeon Holloway (though sometimes, it's true, I'm tempted to head straight back home, nose to bed). Here I am at the Odeon, butter-fingering the chunky glass door, breathing in the carpet shampoo. There is ... something about the recycled air here ... Folksy breaths and gaseous emissions. Stale. I'm instantly sleepy. Oh, I'm so tired. This place should be cross-sectioned. If there is any oxygen left out there on the Holloway Road, it should be redirected at once into this odious Odeon. I declare, here and now, a State of Emergency.

Though I *am* thinking of applying for a job here. Actually. And why not? *I* could wear the red clip-on bow tie and that boiled off-white shirt and look damn good. I'd stand in the door, yawning, lifting my billiard balls through my pockets, watching Demi Moore repeat a gesture twenty-six times. Last week I saw *Star Trek: Generations* an exact five and a half times. I do performances for Drew late at night: I balance precipitously on the lino. I swing backwards, forwards, any-wards, wearing my William-Shatner-I'm-A-Really-Cross-Uncle look. Drew laughs. Which is something I like to hear. She's got *a* laugh! A wheeze with hiccups erupting at exciting intervals. A laugh is something you're stuck with from birth. When I get home I'm going to file that observation under H for *Ha!*

Today they're showing *Just Cause* starring Sean Connery. It's just crap. For the first twenty minutes I am the only punter availing myself of this light show. Then an old guy plops down from the ceiling like a drunk spider, *directly* in front of me. Plop! He smells of urine, alcohol, tab-ends. Why, he's a stinking cliché! As an exercise in forbearance, though, I do not move. I spy, through the fizzy scrag of his head, a jungle scene, spooky webbed trees, chocolate water, the sly side-smile of a crocodile. Connery's screen wife is acting captive in a hut. His kid's tied up there too. Boy (as they say in Amerikay, in the Land of Brunettes), she *is* acting. What a cheesy joy to see! During the hugging denouement, the credits, the old guy turns to me: That Sean Connery, he goes, I like him. I *do*. What a guy. A great guy! Huh? Huh? I smile in a teeth-sucking way. When I've been dreaming of garrotting the git as an experiment in blood spray (see A for Arterial). Instead, I sick up a full bloated stomach-pump smile. The one I use for dole kings and social wankers. I calm myself, wagging a big finger of the imagination. Murderers, Root, *do not* get to heaven.

In the Odeon foyer I blast the remnant of my smile (why waste it) at the girl behind the popcorn chute. She's busy praying. I lip-read her slow prayers, mouth back all her vowels and 'normous consonants. Her glare of holy bored indifference, well, that just about really turns me on. I'm thinking of asking her out for a date too.

What to do in the late afternoon, in the late twentieth century?
I weigh up palms: date? Eat?

I sit in a whitely lit café and eat, for the crack, a soggy
piece of fish. Now, this piece of fish used to sail in an ocean.
No. What is it fish do? They swarm! Or is that bees? This fish
used to swarm like a bee and now here it is attached to my
fork. In my mouth. Down my gob. Nosing wee muscular
shoulders through my innards and . . . Later, it's back in the
sea again. I could say Life=shit, but here I am recycling this
fish bit. Hey, I feel like I'm really engaged here, I'm working!
The guy who served me swabs my table down with a stinking
pair of . . . why, ex-Y-fronts! He has so many – *whoa!* – open
pores in his face I feel myself being . . . sucked into a black
hole; losing my grip on the yellow Formica, off I hurtle.
Trapped by a nose hair.

It's four o'clock. *Where* has the day gone? The screws have
been loosened on the tower clock. They're just flinging time
around. I wind my way back to the flat and, en route, I give
more thought to food. What shall I prepare for my lady wife?
Potato soup, carrot salad, a treacle pud? White. Orange. Light
brown. Hmm, maybe. Last night, yellow, puce, tan. The day
before: cream, moss green, mulberry. She'll be so tired after
work. Oh, she'll be exhausted. All the brats she has to contend
with while I just piss about exclaiming. I'll give her a back
rub . . . I'll do my Sean-Puts-On-His-Very-Clever-Glasses. I
wander into an alley for my big afternoon piss on a wall. I
choose my site carefully, just a little hobby, and make my stain.

And there I see it: the *short cut* to heaven.

No joke. In the alley I spy, up against a spongy pink brick

wall, a tiny bush all a-tremble with pretty daisy flowers. I don't spray that. Who could? Such a friendly daisy baby, such a hopeful baby bud. I turn my back and bathe myself in a tingly sunbeam and, holding my dick all nice (what a green sappy stem!), I spray a mirror up upon the wall. And whoa! Reward. The daisy bush pops up like a pop-up and – ho! A new *Time & Space Continuum*? A stairway to— Heck! It's a hecking *escalator* to heaven! Guarded by . . . oh, blast it, redcoats! Ladybirds! I'm hopelessly outnumbered! I may only drip dry and admire their changing guard, their multileggy patrol.

Oh, depression! I cross the road and, without appearing *too* self-conscious, I attempt to get mown down. There's no one to save. What I wouldn't do for a dreamy toddler innocently at play in the traffic. Where are they now when you need them? I'd wear that phone hood like a hairdryer, spin round double quick and whoosh off through the air, plucking the wee grateful babe out of the way. Would ja believe it! A bus driven by a bus driver with full blown bus driver disease runs me through. Here I am queue jumping the casualties in front of God. Sorry guys, there's only one place left in heaven, and me, Barry, I've got it.

Yeah. Too right. Up the stairs I go. I see Drew in front of me, walking slowly with her satchel weighed down with marking. Smoking in a tired way. Sucking tar. She looks so tired. oh, she looks right done in. What I'm going to do is be *so* good, not talk. I'll just kiss her cheek. Hold all my talk in till end of End of Day. Heck! That is the very *least* I can do.

# *Paper Clips*

It's raining. It's always raining in Romford. Even in the shopping arcade and in the subway tunnels it's raining. There's rain strung down the strobe lighting like dirty diamanté. Outside, where the rain, in the main, is, it's berried on the trees grey and glimmerless. It slashes and it curtains and it drops down in nails. It tries to be other, but it's rain.

In the morning I walk through Romford market and buy myself a hard banana and a piece of Tupperware. For some reason the colour yellow and a piece of Tupperware cheer me up. I dawdle in the Pound Stretcher shop but see nothing worth stretching 50p. Slowly, I approach the rotting tooth of Warner B jutting out from the pavement and, right on cue, each nerve in my body shoots its mouth and goes, No! Emelda! *Do not* go in there. Oh, Emelda, there *is* blue sky somewhere and a frothy playful sea. *You* could be splashing in salty sea water. *You* could be bathed in an orange water light. Oh, do not be a slave. But it is my fate to find myself sealed in the coffin lift, rising above Romford, above the water line, with the maniacal sound of lift dentistry ringing in my ears. I wake from death. I pound on the doors like a body buried by mistake. The doors squeeze open, and in for a squeeze steps Mr Andrew Head. The sound of my obedience:

159

'Good Morning Mr Head.' My sing-song voice like a telephonist's

'Hello Emelda, you're . . . looking . . .'

Don't do it Mr Head. Mr Charisma you ain't.

'. . . Gar-*rate*!' Ahh, the silly frump. We rise together in the stink of his silliness. His Klingon forehead pops out sweat. And why are there so few, not enough, not enough by half, female serial killers? The strain, that *strained* female quality of mercy! I hear myself snigger politely. When I had him *right there, squirming*. I crash through the ruffled corridors holding my head. I stagger to my desk muttering and whimpering repentance. I press, accidentally, a button on my PC and send fifty thousand ginger balaclavas rocketing off to a gas explosion in Bahrain.

The young Teaboy, son of Sinister Teaboy, puts his head round the door and – like he's barking, like he's really barking *mad* – burps.

There is something wrong, *so wrong* with all the men who work for Warner B. Medically, physically, psychically. Mr Andrew Head, as *clearly* demonstrated (day in, day out), is a Klingon fool and cannot even clean his teeth properly. They wear an unexportable coat of grey-green plaque. There's the twin mailboys and one has a limp and the other has something sinister up with his ears. The blond Teaboy, I've noticed, is careful not to go out in the wind, hair like frozen butter curls.

There's the Sales and Marketing force who share dwarfism, oafism and halitosis.

There's Publicity and Export and these guys share vampirism, wigism and scaly scabrous skin. There's Maintenance and

Cleanliness which is an ironic title. Which must be the company ha ha. They wear tan-coloured coats like onion skins, they hug, under their arms, warm sweaty onion rings the size of rugby balls. They *reek*.

There's us, 'the girls'.

And. There's nothing wrong with us.

We're a happy–unhappy Crew trapped here on the Starship Warner B. I light a fag and wander back into the corridors to start my morning rip at the walls. I see, dimly outlined, my Crew start their morning rip at the walls too. In the corridors, the light is raining dirty blue. The thin partitions flap and buckle and flap back in the breeze from the shrunken window frames. Romford rain sits on the window ledge and spits in. Eyes spy. Here, at Warner B, eyes glaze out from the torn and tattered remains, the damp Technicolor posters of beefy babes. Here, imperfections on fulsome and lonesome display, are the Commie pin-up stars from 1947, '54, '68 . . . Old girls set for ever in pale powder-blue. Bad bottle blondes, black at the roots like rotten haystacks, soft-skinned like old fruits. Yellow, pancaked, mustachioed, sad. Clearly, our sisters had shorter forearms then; cream stretch marks curve their bellies. Spots hill their faces. We, my Crew, Natalie and the young sweet Cherry, routinely tear them down on our solidarity march to the loo, to the tea trolley, on the watch for Warner Baxter Jones, ripping away in the mornings, clawing away at a strip of poster leg, peeling away a toothy pout, a crusty orange shoulder, scooping out an occasional pretty eye, a crunchy-nippled breast in a crochet turquoise bikini bra. Someone – Klingon Andrew Head perhaps? The Sinister

Teaboy? Son of Sinister Teaboy? . . . it could be any *one* of a host, a gallery of reeky misfit men – slaps them straight back up again, stealing around the building with paste on his hands.

Someone imports posters to wind us up.

*Why* am I surprised?

Back in my office I lift a heavy tear-lashed eyelid and see, by the window, through my groggy sparkle, the Warner B catalogue on its plywood altar, rustling away in the contaminated breeze, pages glossing through its garish and loathsome display: splashy porous orange, trashy cerise. Dollop of paisley. Pease-pudding-green . . . In another life, long ago, three long years ago, I used to wonder who on earth *could* supply those shops that sell tangerine-frilled 100% polyester (declared as a boast) blouses? Or them there shiny Toldeo-red ruffled shirts that will never need ironing, which can only be destroyed if held *directly* in the heat of an atomic explosion? Warner B does. I do. I deal in the import and export of clothes you don't want to touch. Stuff that makes your fingers recoil into fists. Not a natural fibre in sight. This stuff is guaranteed to live on with the insects . . . Acrylic sherbet-pink knee-length skirts the exact shade of a Ski strawberry yoghurt or a black poodle's dick . . . A suedette car coat with fur lapels which, alternatively, you could line your immersion heater with . . . Tan-coloured suits with flared raspberry panelling. Yellow denim jackets with faux pony elbow patches. This stuff will never be retro. It comes in bulk, warehoused for decades, in soft cellophane. It sells slowly to blind people, to the tactilely challenged. We, my Crew, Natalie and the young sweet Cherry, send the backlist, the seriously unnatural, to places where walls were, where wars and/or diseases have broken out. It's for people who need to be covered and don't much care. It's a tax write-off. Warner B like to target people in shock and dress them down.

I tell myself I am not responsible for this. I am enslaved.

In my office I stand, at last, to greet my two-girl Crew, breathing in our bad-love-contaminated air. That is the one thing wrong with us. Love. *He*, Mr Warner Baxter Jones, *will not love us*. He will not. That is our distinguishing mark. We're all split up with, or snapped off from, we're ragged with cuts. We're the hazel sticks *he* has nearly chewed off a branch: still a bit dewy, a bit bleedy, hanging on. All day we track *his* footsteps above our heads, anticipate *his* every move. Now he is . . . stretching his arms . . . Now he is standing beside his white statue smoking and stroking a frozen marble limb. Now he is lying on the white leather couch where once he lay with . . . me, Emelda, fat Natalie, the young sweet Cherry.

There's something – so very *wrong* with all of us. We're stuck here in Romford, in thrall, IN ugly love.

I say '*Good* Morning!' And Cherry sighs. She's a (relatively) new recruit to Warner B. To this pain-processing plant. I don't know much about her personal history, her private route to pain, but I do know a serious heartbreak. You don't expect to draw another breath. The way the chest goes still.

Cherry stands by the window, rubbing a porthole into the grime. I see a cloud out there loaded with squid's ink. 'Hey, cloud!' I yell. 'Squirt it on Romford!'

The smell of warm vanilla turns me round. It's Natalie. Fat

Nat shimmying towards us in her extra epidermis, holding out our big breakfast plate of home-baked cake. We circle the plate like three vampires savouring fresh blood pie: we sink our fangs through a nail's thickness of coconut dust, raspberry jam, deep yellow sponge. Jammily smile. Nat smiles ecstatically back. She's into oral happiness now. She wants me and Cherry to find happiness this sweet way too. Fill our void. If Warner Baxter Jones won't love us, food can. Fat, Natalie glows as though *stuffed* with liquid nitrogen. Her smile anaesthetized. When she used to be *thin* as a *pair of dusty black tights. Spit* smoke and expletives, *howl* her love. Now, she sails through the floors, new cells glowing, growing, brightly packed, her glossy helmet of hair snug upon her head. She sails, becalmed along the ruffled corridors, in a spectrum of red. Splat! Comes *splattering* splat-gore back along the walls when Warner Baxter Jones blanks on by.

Warner Baxter Jones descends in the lift. His glossy forehead. His hair combed straight back above his ears, tight as wings.

Hear us *die*!

This morning we have a consignment of wide-lapelled block-printed shirts we could send to Japan where an earthquake has recently sucked in the centre of a city.

'Imagine,' Cherry says, 'the buildings shaking like cardboard, falling like cards. Towers of pinky grey dust rising . . . It doesn't bear thinking about.'

I don't bother thinking about it. Cherry does. Cherry is seriously empathetic. She cries when she hears the wail of an ambulance. She's crying now. She flicks through the catalogue, pushing her red ribbony hair behind her ears. She wants to send them 'something *really* nice', but today it's the ugly shirts or lilac sweatsuits encrusted with plastic lemon drops.

'Look, we can't do that to the Japanese,' Cherry says.

'We *can*,' Natalie says, fountaining sugar into her tea – as though from her finger! As though she's just nozzled off a nail! She had an aunt taken prisoner at Sumatra, Indonesia. That aunt has never recovered. She screams at Japanese tourists in Oxford Street. We pass the morning discussing punishments. Which is the worse colour punishment: lilac lemon or limey green? We send the encrusted lilac sweatsuits.

The clock hands creak round. And we enter, with jerking movements, the dead zone of afternoon.

We should *leave* Warner Bax now, but, we're held in his spell.

Warner Baxter Jones moves above our heads, light like light. Now, and now he is smoking. Now he is crossing to the door. Walking down the corridor. Descending in the lift. I turn my head and see, in the corner, a wall I've made from cataracts: three years of sturdy Tupperware. I see, in my mind, an itemized vat of banana skins. A day-by-day blast of yellow *cheer me up!*

Cherry and Natalie grab their headphones. They plug out their pain. I stare out at the stained canvas sky. The rain is pain. A plane passes. A plane whizzes the hell out of Romford. I see an undercarriage glint Morse code: f . . . r . . . e . . . e . . . dom? No. F-R-E-E-T-H-E-M. I hear Natalie move a consignment of fleeced yellow gents' shirts from Bosnia to

Chetchnya. Cherry backtails four racks of plum and goose-berry men's slacks from the former GDR to the former Yugoslavia.

They're both crying. I'm crying too but I'm so used to tears I no longer feel wet. I feel myself tip ahead with tears. It's one tear too far. Someone has to do something. I leave the office as I'm the girl to do it.

In the corridors my neat uniform of pale-biscuit-beige blurs. The old babes flap and agitate along the wall.

Warner Baxter Jones. Warner ... Baxter ... Jones. He smells of musk, honey-coloured like the air around his head, sticky with beeswax. One touch and you're stuck. Is it natural? Pharmaceutically produced like nerve gas? Is it his fault that there is no visible chink in his perfection? That we serve him like lovesick dogs? Perhaps perfection *is* his imper-fection? Not a hair out of place. His smooth moves. His smooth ... The idea grows parallel with lust, multiples like a cancer cell, *is*, suddenly, tumour-shaped huge: *if* I had evid-ence of imperfection to share, this pain ... I am outside his office, fighting my swoon in his high altitude air. I am *in*side his office.

And I do not recall this ultra, flashing white. The walls are white ... they beat light at me, white cabbage light, it's like being trapped in the heat-beat of a butterfly. And, through the beat, I feel, deeper even than the steady pump of love, I feel the chill thrill of his calculation.

The carpet sinks me into depths of white. Up to my knees in white ... The walls are white, the ceiling, the standard lamps, the statuary, the long-remembered dentless leather couch (where once we lay joined through gaps in our clothing. He lay there, likewise, with Natalie. Likewise, the young sweet Cherry. He will lie there again with a new initiate. *Pain*.). I hold my guts. Double up: *pain*. The desk is blonde. I sit on the swivel chair and feel myself expand in this space. And swivel at the shades of pale. I pull drawers open. There, perfectly, and, I . . . see now, I see now, anally aligned, a stack of creamy-white paper. A stack of Warner Baxter Jones cards. Pens, the silver nibs in tune one with the other. A tray of assorted office paraphernalia. A bright tray of paper clips. I feel the palm of my hand grow warm . . . warmer. Hot. I push a button and one hundred thousand scrolled up Technicolor Commie babes drop from the ceiling and fall from the walls. They plead on the floor, their pink pearly frosted mouths gulp like spilled goldfish: Free . . . No. *Kill* us.

I begin to string the paper clips into daisy chains and mark out my trail . . . down the corridor, into the lift shaft, to the fuselage of my Crew ship door.

## Epilogue

The rain falls down on Romford in glittering breaking chains.

*Closing Time*

'I remember when all this were . . . fields.' With his gloved Viking paw the Viking indicates their greasy view of the city: an intersection; lorries, buses, cars, all running into each other like strands in a plait.

'I remember when', Peggy says, cranking down the industrial toaster, 'I had a job with prospects.'

She sinks her long black rubber gloves into a bowl of slimy washing up.

For two pounds an hour cash, she, Dr Peggy Jones, fries bright plate-loads of yellow food; shiny hairless splat burns on her pale green forearms. She is beginning, in spongy middle age, to sprout out sideways like a spud: a spongy speaking spud, reciting all day Cod and chips, Quarter of chicken 'n' chips, Bubble 'n' chips. Chips . . . chips. Reciting, all day: Tea, coffee, large or small? To have here or take away? What, take away? Toast?

Peggy drifts across to the toaster.

There is something . . . drifting along the base of the industrial toaster, something grey and furled above the crumbs like under-bed fur. Peggy cranks up the lever and two tiny toasted pink paws appear, too late for prayers. Peggy shakes.

Peggy shakes the scorched body out; mechanically notes contusions to the ears, 95 per cent burns, the long sheenless tail shredding like rope. Her tiny spud-black eyes monitor the tremor of her hands on the flip bin. Better. They used to shake all day. *She* used to shake all day. The ketchup in the gagged plastic bottles once pulsed out blood. She'd hold carving knives above the chickens, the bacon backs, the greasy racks of lamb, hack, hack at cheese: where, once, she *cut* with *precision*, frilled skin, *incisively* scythed; peeped beneath a tarpaulin of slack belly flesh, scooped out polycystic ovaries as she now scoops at barely poached eggs. Dr Peggy Jones. Her nerves are shot. She sees them shot down one after the other like ducks. Dr Peggy Jones. Surgeon. Kitchen hand.

Peggy looks up. Four minutes to six. Four minutes before the story of her recent tragic history kicks in, waiting, each evening, like a mugger. The light in the café is a dripping watery brown. Drizzling lime round the door. The Viking, Harry, sits with his back to her, neckless, dew-sodden like a sea hulk; spuming solid blue smoke. Somehow, just before closing time, Harry creeps in. Peggy sees other shadows dancing around the door. Vikings shoe-shuffling their queer standstill dance. She sees Vikings everywhere now where she saw none before: loping round corners in their floor-length coats; their whole held together by knotty belts, gapped like vertebrae, like sideways spines, moving like *Ow!* There's an axe stuck in my 'ead. Just enough change in their pockets for one cup of tea. 'We're *closed*,' Peggy mouths. The Vikings slowly react: scratch, shake their bashed yellow knuckles, mime through a pillar-box slit in their heads. Harry sighs along with her, shakes his own grizzled, roughly hoed head. Peggy pours him the dregs of the pot; a lukewarm cup of orange tea, cuts a thickly margarined slice of bread, plops it all down on the sudsy table. Turns off the lights. Tells him to Drink up Harry. Please don't give her a hard time.

She means, don't talk Harry. She's asking for a miracle: stop the winter, don't let it rain.

Bring Nurse Calhoun back from the dead.

Don't talk Harry. She swabs at the tables with a foul-smelling floor cloth.

Harry talks, 'Why, Miss Peggy, this bright slab of bread, it's why. . .' He turns it, pleasantly struck, flings the last of the limey traffic light back, marvels at its high yellow summer sheen, 'why, it's like a field of rape.'

'Polyunsaturates,' Peggy barks.

In the kitchen she pulls the fridge door open and finds the morgue. Dry white ice. Nurse Calhoun's wrinkled toe-tagged feet. She sinks her forehead down on to a cold slab of sealed Cheddar cheese and begins to weep.

*

She lived in her high-rise flat *and* on a trestle bed in the high-rise hospital. The hospital car park, blackly tarmacadamed, lay twinkling far far below like an upside-down sky. She hears her own purposeful footsteps tapping over the stars. Behind her Nurse Calhoun's heavier tread. Around them the silent humped and grey dew-jewelled cars. Nurse Calhoun's hand on her shoulder turning her round. She lives Nurse Calhoun turning her round.

In the theatre, robed, the cool blue light making their masks and her kirby grips whiter than white, and the trays of instruments glitter and shift like shallow desperate fish, Nurse Calhoun's elbow pressing into her back. He whispered, 'Dr Jones, I love . . .' Because of the mask she heard, 'A wuf. I *wuv* . . .'

But she, busy Dr Peggy Jones, had no time at all for love.

\*

'Time was. . .' Harry says, addressing the brown café glass, where the flow of the traffic flickers like a blurred tobacco-soaked cine-film; his half-plucked neckless head bobs, he gives Peggy side glimpses of his pumice-stone-shaped nose, 'Aye, time was when a fella could think the one thought all day, let it glide in the head, aye, like the flight of a fly. No impediments. No impedimenta. Well, no buildings . . .'

Peggy picks up her anorak and makes, chin up, for the door. Sometimes, if she can just *slip* . . . She smells the mugger, muggy now, close. She'll need a knife to *hack*, hack her way home. 'Please,' she whimpers, 'Harry, please . . . just . . . go.' Her fingers tremble, press down invisible piano keys.

'And trees!' Harry yelps. 'They had . . . age then, and . . . something else, ingredients that escape me now. Those ones out there,' he points to a barely visible line of branchless green, 'Miss Peggy, wouldn't that auld baldy head remind you now of an ailing propped-up spring onion?'

'Shut *up*,' Peggy yells. She feels the mugger on her, snatching the present. *Cosh!*

\*

Nurse Calhoun's furneral. Hot summer. She wore her best black winter coat, smelling of mothball . . . formaldehyde. Tight: its shrinkage centimering across her back. Sweat wormed on her back. For *she* would not wear a summer dress. *Nobody goes to funerals in summer dresses!* She hid out in the copper trees, in a wide copper splash, and wept. Through her personal muslin screen she saw Nurse Calhoun's wife in a short summer frock, the eight sons of Calhoun. His parents standing short and erect like barely etched pottery folk. Two humps of black glossy earth. A half-moon of hospital staff. A space where she should be. A Dr Jones-shaped absence. Her high-rise fell down. The high-rise hospital imploded. She saw the silent debris suspended over her head. She ran in shaking terror to a café. This café. Read, as she ravenously slit through food, a sign that read ELP! WANTED. MATURITY PRIFFED.

'My life is shit without you,' Nurse Calhoun had said. She saw a pile of steaming tubular shit.

Snap.

\*

'Time was,' Harry said. 'We're *closed*,' Peggy says. But she says this uselessly, backing over to the counter, pulling a lever so Harry disappears for a while in a gust of chocolate steam. She's so permanently cold inside. Cold as a rose, old as a stone. Dead as a door . . . Nurse Calhoun gassed himself in the family Volvo estate. His face red as a rose, abloom from the carbon monoxide fumes. She heard the loud chugg chugg *boom* of the Volvo estate, the dark grey-suit coloured air piling up against the garage roof. Harry's voice . . .

'Green? It were that green. It were. . .' He frowns for twenty minutes, stirring his one inch of cold tea, '. . . it were emerald green. When you put your foot on land it were . . . being on the sea so long, in the longboat like, your own blood doesn't tend to flow, it undulates, slops up right against your cheek. Land were like. . .' his spoon rattles, '. . . well it were like. . .' Minutes tick . . .

'Cushions,' Peggy says, pouring more chocolate out into two chipped mugs. 'Duvets? Silk velvet? Slumberland beds?'

'Aye,' Harry says, sipping, 'it were cushio*ny* but it had spring. A fella didn't have to walk under his own steam at all in them there days. No. The land sprung you up under your feet. From here to where Islington is now, it would take me then about,' his chest fills, 'about seven steps.'

'Aye,' Peggy says, bitterly, slopping Harry's cup down, 'when I were lass.'

*

'You *beautiful* girl,' Nurse Calhoun gasped in the hotel room.

She hissed, 'OK, we'll do it *just once*.' She couldn't, literally, operate. Waves of heat came from Nurse Calhoun, his radar rippling through her breasts and groin. The patient, sectioned, lay on the operating table obscenely sexualized. 'OK,' she said, '*once*.' Though she was lit all the way up. She were, she *was*, standing in the orange glow from the gas fire, drying her hair, surprised in her underwear, bending *in her tights*! feeling her fatty cells in a jig with each drying strand of her hair. She was forty-five years old.

'Oh, you are a *beautiful* girl.'

*

'Aye, a fella could rove in them days. You would walk from Mare Street to Victoria Coach Station and you could have a cup of tea and two women on the way. Aye, you could stop off in a tattie field for lunch, scoop your hole, light a fire. Baked potatoes. Steaming it would be. Not like that there. . .' the paw paws where a blob of colour, a pink neon light blinks, '. . . SPUD U LIKE. Two seconds on a plate and the heat's gone. Aye, you'd bake two extra ones for your pockets, warm your hands. And rain. Look at that!' Rain sprinkles against the glass like spit. 'It used to rain like silk! A fella would welcome it. And when I say silk I mean runnels of it. It were. . .' The spoon taps.

'Lovely. Delicious,' Peggy supplies, stacking up chairs, 'wonderful.'

'It were a glorious *gift*! The sun would come out and it were in them days a wet sun and it would come out,' he plaits his fingers together, slides one palm slowly against the butt of the other, 'and there would be, oh, this great shimmering and this immense . . . unfurling, like you wouldn't know your spine had been bent and you'd be straightening yourself up.'

'Harry,' Peggy calls. She sees, dimly now, his hulked shape smoking through the scorched chair legs, his doused volcano.

An ambulance shrieks by and streaks him two-tone red. 'Harry?'

'I'm here, lass. Aye, you'd need a time to tell. And where the Mile End Road is now a fella could pluck, as though from the air,' his paw waves airily, 'the fruit hanging down from the trees, and it would be like heavy orbs . . . a kind of mess inside . . . and the juicy stuff of it would run over your beard or, with just a few twigs and a fast eye, you'd trap the hares in the field, stick a stick up through the anus and mouth, peel off its fur into these here very same mitten gloves. You'd wear what you'd eat. Aye . . .'

At the counter, in the flashing dark, Peggy scrapes at the frying pans with a moan, lifts out the cold yellow-eyed eggs and a slab of bubbled fry. Crumples shrivelled bacon rinds into a paper bag.

'A carry-out, Harry. Then-you-out.' Peggy looks from the bacteria-rich heart-attack fare to Harry's mildly shivering stack. Slowly, takes from the fridge a bloodied pummelled steak. The air starts to sizzle and pop. Onions caramelize. Steak and garlic pump out fumes. The arms of her anorak sponge up soft globules of fat.

Harry lifts his voice above the fry, 'Aye, the Mile End Road then, Miss Peggy, it were, it were a winding bed of berries, beady ones, rubies. It were like the dropped necklace of a giant giantess. And sometimes, aye, you'd hear her footsteps and the drag of her awesome evening gown pulling down trees and transplanting hamlets. Aye, the sound of her thunder would send us – anything with wings or four or two legs – aye would send us . . .'

'Scurrying,' Peggy says, definitely, supplying the grease-speckled plate. 'Go home, Harry.' Outside, the plait of traffic is lit now like fireflies, long entwined beams run the café through.

The Viking swallows in the dark. 'Aye, the air full of wings and strange shrieks and cries.'

'Go home' Peggy says.

'Home,' says Harry.

'Home,' Peggy echoes. She sees herself stepping into the tiny coffin lift, transported up, up into the high-rise limbo of her flat. She sinks down beside Harry and sobs.

'Aye,' Harry says. 'I recall one time now, and I'm going further back, rowing the longboat in the Thames. We did not know it was the Thames then. Well, we did not know what it was. There was sickness. Carrion crows followed us. Our great creaking hulk. We could see them circling in outline, patiently beaked on the great piebald skies. The air was . . .'

*

The sheets were peaked; frothed like egg whites. Nurse Calhoun lay asleep face down on the hotel bed. She watched him knowing that here, in a rented room, lay her last man. Then he lay, too tired for sleep, in the blue Nurses' Lounge. She smelt, from the doorway, the intimate half-lit coffee-sock air, saw his fag end arc away from his lightly boned head. Stood in the doorway, framed in her resolve, choked.

*

'Aye, it were lonely, lonesome. The bone-chill air, the vapour on the water thickly furred like mould, the water outside slurping with the movement of a single oar and ploppings like the plop of a lizard from a rock or . . . and I looked at my fellow fellas and they were slumped grey and there were not a sound of breathing from them though all muscles moved with the pull of the boat. And the longboat made up waves as we moved sideways, aye, the waves rocking up full of . . . a dark peaked intent like logs of crocodiles and there I was where Canary Wharf is now with its one red sleepless eye, naked in a longboat with ten dead men.'

'Dead,' Peggy says.

'Aye, Miss Peggy, they were. I were lonely then. And my boy, I had a son, Gregor. I recall his sprout of carrot-coloured hair. Aye, Gregor . . . his milky-blue chest, the nut-nipples on it like clenched eyes, closed faster than eyes. It were as though he died twice. I tipped him over the side. I carry the dread image of him like a picture postcard inside my head.'

Harry stills Peggy's piano-playing hands.

'I carry the dread image,' Peggy whispers.

'The dead . . .' Harry says. 'Miss Peggy, any jam roly-poly?'

'Aye.' Peggy says, standing, moving backwards through the dusk.

'Aye.' Harry says, through the clatter of pans, 'I kept busy then, wondering. Aye, we were all full of wonder then and it were a gift to be alive. And in them days you could see a person without distraction. You could see their approach for miles. And they were framed in a great sky and the only obscurity were the strands of grass on their feet. You had time enough to tell then. You could stop or walk on by. You walked then till you died. And oftentimes I had occasion to bury a fella at the side of the road. And he'd be no more than a sack of bones. I buried me one off the Whitechapel road and others, I recall, a tall man and a taller woman in no more than rags, long dead, still in a lipless kiss. I laid them together. Her hair a loose coil and still yellow underneath. It were . . . dappled black and yellow like a mess of hay. There's a tree now in Bedford Square. And sometimes in the autumn, in a certain pinkish light, I believe I see her standing stretching up slowly underneath her hair. Aye.'

'Aye,' Peggy says. Outside, the night is pre-dawn blue. A lime washes in from the stream of cars. Puddles slap against the gutters like waves. Peggy leans above Harry, in the hot jam-scented air, falling forward like a figurehead. She feels the lino move. She looks at Harry's head, and sees a planet there for fleas . . . all the fleas are dancing there. They hop about on springy hairy knees. They leap.

Dr Peggy Jones lifts her hands and pinching deftly, operates air.